Crystal's Unicorn,

The Dark Prince and the Angel Chronicles

By Jeannie S. Wise

This book is a work of fiction. Names, characters, businesses, organizations, places, events and incidents either are the product of the author's imagination or are used fictitiously. Any resemblance to actual persons, living or dead, events, or locales is entirely coincidental. Cover designed by Jeannie S. Wise

First edition January 2015

The Dark Prince and the Angel Chronicles   1

Thanks

Acknowledgments

This book is dedicated to my close friends and family; those that encouraged thank you and to those that just shook there heads at me, here is your official raspberry from me to you. I do love you all.

Thank you to my wonderful friends that helped me along the way with edits, suggestions and just listening to me bang my head against the desk. A special thank you to Laura Ranger, Marcella Prybil and Kimberly Mitchell for wearing the editor hats. I hope you know how much I love and appreciate you. And my BETA readers are awesome.

My idol Author Torie James, your continued inspiration and encouragement never ceases to amaze me…. Much love.

Thank you for reviews and guidance to some great authors, Laura Ranger, Stacy Von Haegert and Torie James (If you don't know them you need to read one of their books NOW)

My model and muse for Michael/Franco, Francesco Abbatangelo. You know how much I appreciate you my friend.

If you don't know him go visit his Facebook page right now https://www.facebook.com/pages/Franco-Abbatangelo . And follow him Instagram http://instagram.com/fatangelo33

The original photograph of Francesco taken by Mr. Hans Duengel . He and his lovely wife Britta do the most incredible work. PLEASE visit their website Www.DuEngel-ART.de

Models of Bonaventura and Crystal courtesy of Shutterstock. http://www.shutterstock.com/index-in.mhtml

Most but not all descriptions of the nine worlds from The Project Gutenberg EBook of Myths of the Norsemen, by H. A. Guerber. As well as quoted poems to read more visit @ http://www.gutenberg.org/

Prologue

THERE HAVE BEEN MANY STORIES OVER THE CENTURIES, some true, but most myth of how the Vampire came to exist in our world. Listen carefully for I am about to tell you the truth of which I am certain.

Before the dawn of man, there were realms beyond your ability to imagine. The realms I mention are but a few of what came to be known as the nine worlds of Norse Mythology, but myth they are not.

The Archangels Vettorio and Michael were Odin's favorite pair of angels, often selected by him for special assignments. They were both once looked upon as second only to the gods themselves. Revered by lesser angels and regarded by demons. Even the giant fire demon, Surt honored the pair with respect when they called on him in Muspelheim.

For countless millennia, the pair roamed as inseparable brothers keeping vigil over all of the nine realms. They had a bond like none other. The newly created Earth soon became a playground where they could escape from their other-worldly responsibilities and find solace in the vast openness and silence. It wasn't until after the creation of humankind, or should I say woman that things began to go horribly wrong.

Vettorio had found favor from the female called Lilith. She lusted after the handsome angel with the beautiful bright blue eyes. Becoming increasingly jealous of Michael and his bond with Vettorio, she set out to seduce Vettorio and have him to herself. It took nearly one hundred years for her plan to come to fruition, but that it did.

Despite Michael's constant warnings, Vettorio lost all resolve and lay with Lilith. Once she had him caught in the thralls of her passion, he became a slave to her flesh. The angel had never experienced sins of the flesh and Lilith was a master at pleasuring him. Their physical relationship became more euphoric than anything he had ever known. Vettorio slowly turned away from his brother angel and every belief he had followed for tens of thousands of years.

Lilith had also secretly taken up with a lesser angel called Baldassare. He was so in love with her that he followed her blindly. Though jealous of Vettorio, he never dared stand against the archangel. He was merely a baby compared to Vettorio's age and powers. When Lilith was cautioned to refrain from her sexual escapades by the council of the gods, she took a stand against the gods. Thinking she was above reproach, she refused to comply with their wishes. Baldassare was the first to side with her. Not wanting to give her up Vettorio reluctantly went along with her defiance and lay with her despite warnings to free himself of her.

The three were held in Niflheim, while their fate was decided. This holding place was a cold, endlessly dark, misty world of snowscapes and was once home of the frost giant Ymir, and ruled by the death goddess

Hela, daughter of Loki. In some accounts this was the last of nine worlds, a place into which the most evil souls of the mortal dead were confined, subjected to hardships and torture before reaching the region of death (Hell).

Situated below one of the roots of the world tree, Niflheim contains a well, Hvergelmir, a bubbling spring from which all cold rivers were born. It is the original source of all living creatures and the great dragon Nidhug guards it. Scampering continually up and down the branches and trunk of the tree was the squirrel Ratatosk (branch-borer). He was the typical gossip, and passed his time repeating to the dragon below the remarks of the eagle above, and vice versa, in the hope of stirring up ill will between them. The world tree called Yggdrasil grew up into the sky and draws water from Hvergelmir. It is said that only the wood from Yggdrasil has the power to destroy the vampires pure in bloodline and the place where it grows on Earth is a closely guarded secret.

The three were summoned from Niflheim and led to Gladsheim by Thor. They stood in judgment before the gods in Gladsheim. Odin was seated on his throne, Hildskialf with his feet resting upon a foot stool of the purest gold. The two Ravens, Hugin (thought) and Munin (memory) were perched on his shoulders while his wolves Geri and Freki sat at his feet. The twelve seats of the Aesir were filled by the council of the gods while the twenty-four Asynjur (goddesses) gathered at the bidding of Odin in the great hall.

Vettorio was the only one who spoke with any remorse. Had it not been for Odin and his great fondness of him they might have met their demise that day. But in what he considered an act of mercy he bargained with the council of the gods for a less severe punishment. But had he an idea of what punishment the council would invoke on his once friend Vettorio, he might have not left the final decision to the council.

Lilith was sent to Vanaheim, the home of the Vanir gods where she was to serve as a slave. Only the gods know where Vanaheim is, or how it looks. However, the

Vanir are masters of sorcery and magic and Lilith absorbed every bit of knowledge she possibly could, growing into the most powerful sorceress of all time then and now.

Lilith escaped after the sixth century of her sentence, making her way to Muspelheim: Land of Fire, home to all things born of fire including dragons and demons where the giant Surt rules. It is foretold that it is he who will ride against Asgard upon his most fierce dragon carrying a flaming sword, turning the home of the gods into an inferno thus the end of our world. This is where Baldassare had been banished to exist among the lava, flames and soot that flourish there. He embraced the darkness of the demons there and became filled with evil, growing into a powerful demon himself. Once free, the two fled together to Svartalfheim, the home of the dark elves where they were hidden in the murky darkness of that realm with the assistance of Lucifer.

His curse was twofold. Vettorio had been stripped of his wings and cursed to wander the Earth for eternity as what would come to be known as vampire. Mankind

12

had rapidly become such a disappointment to the gods. There were those who mistakenly thought Vettorio would rid the Earth of the malcontent humans. He was the first, the original King of darkness from which all vampires were born. It is told that he was a tortured soul, sulking for the first hundred years of his exile alone on Earth longing for Lilith and the company of his brother angel. Alone, he would roam the lush rolling hills and hike the Alps where he and Michael had frolicked like children, laughing and singing or just sitting on a mountain top bathing in the sun conversing with one another. He lost his grace and his wings but had held fast to a ray of humanity.

Vettorio witnessed as humankind grew and flourished around him. Unable to bare his solitude any longer, he created three daughters, the first being Selena, who had been his lover for some time before her sister's, Aslaug and Judit were created in the hope of calming the storm that was Selena. Aslaug and Judit were strong, powerful vampires yet they had both maintained a semblance of their humanity and were known to often show a motherly compassion for their creations. They tried to be sisters to Selena, but she would have no part of it and resented their mere existence. The very thought of sharing Vettorio's affection with anyone sent Selena into a murderous rage in 588 AD that lasted nearly two hundred years. Paired with the actual plague inflicted upon the ungrateful masses by the gods, close to half of Europe's population was wiped out by 700 AD. Only the faithful of the Far North were spared.

Vettorio fueled rumors that these deaths were all a result of a second wave of the Plague of Justinian to cover up her indiscriminant slaughter of the humans. Selena was a problem child for Vettorio from the day she awoke a vampire. She was jealous, willful, stubborn and defiant. Although she constantly broke his laws and risked exposure of his race, Vettorio could not bring himself to allow her to be executed. Any harm to her was forbidden. He couldn't look at her without seeing the beautiful innocent that had once shared his bed and warmed his cold dead heart.

Even after her rage had calmed, Selena enjoyed a cat and mouse game with her victims that more often than not ended with her ripping their hearts out for sport. She turned only a select group of males and females that she found sexually attractive and wished to keep as playmates. Turning her nose up at her sisters she made her home away from them and the king; sharing a small castle in Germany with the group of sexual deviants she had created. This is the group of vampires from which the nightmarish blood lust vampire was born.

Michael had been forbidden any contact with Vettorio upon his exile. Over the centuries, he went before the council repeatedly seeking mercy for Vettorio. His pleas were rejected time after time. The only compassion to be found in the council of the gods was from Odin and Thor. In the tenth century of Vettorio's exile, Odin followed Michael from the council meeting, "Walk with me and we shall come to an understanding of what will and will not be permitted." Odin spoke in soft, deliberate tones as he pulled the hood of his blue mantle with its grey speckles up over his dark curly hair. His mantle hung wide across his massive shoulders and broad chest. Michael felt the corners of his mouth curving up into a half smile, the first he had managed since Vettorio was lost to him. He looked attentively into the Allfather's eyes in silent reverence. "I am sorrowed by his fate Michael, but Vettorio will never be offered a chance at redemption. His destiny has been sealed and that you cannot alter even though his cohorts seemed to have escaped their fate. It has been agreed upon that you shall be permitted to visit ertho (Earth) again for short periods of time. You may seek out Vettorio's company. Converse with him as you wish, but do not allow yourself to become involved in his darkness." Odin stopped walking, placing a huge hand on Michael's shoulder. "Make no mistake, the council did not find favor in my suggestion of this lightly. This offer is made only for your sake and the one who shall be born. It is fated he is to be guided by you. Should you stray from the path lain before you that door will be closed to you forever." Odin gave Michael a look that warned him it was ill advised to ask questions.

Michael swore a blood oath, his palm pierced upon the tip of Odin's sacred spear, Gungnir. He would spend half of his time in the Earthly realm and when the time came he would watch over and guide this yet unknown child until he grew into a man. Wiping a tear from his cheek Michael nodded in agreement. "I wish to thank you Odin. I know without you on my side, this would not be." Embracing the Allfather of the gods that towered over him in size with his wings opened to their full length, Michael felt a glimpse of joy in his heart again.

1

Soul Mates

Bozen, Italy

December 0817

VETTORIO GLIDED THROUGH THE DRIVING SNOW, SENSING HIS WAY, more than seeing it. Even with his superior sight, the night sky being darkened by the storm had resulted in zero visibility. It was thick and murky and he could feel the weight of the storm hanging around him. Had he not paused to brush

18

away the drop of blood clinging to his lower lip, he might not have noticed her sitting on the church steps. He could hear tiny whimpers. Getting a bit closer, but not too close, he could see that her chest rose and fell struggling to breathe in the air that was so cold her tears were forming ice crystals on the edges of her long lashes.

Althea was drawn up in a little package shivering, sobbing in silence. Her long curls wrapped around her shoulders forming little copper colored bowls catching the snowflakes.

Vettorio found himself strangely drawn to the tiny figure in an unfamiliar way that made him twitch. He could barely make her out as female through the blizzard beating down against his face. Yet, he was drawn even nearer for a better view of this mysterious creature. She looked up; a faint flash of moonlight between clouds against her face illuminated a pair of emerald green doe eyes. Vettorio stopped behind the church's stone wall and watched her. He had the most compelling urge to scoop her up and take her off to his bed. Not to feed, but to comfort her, not to merely seduce, but make love to her. *Oh hell no*, he flashed in the opposite direction. In moments, he was pacing miles away in a wooded area near Lake Garda. He was out of sight of those damned sad, intoxicating eyes that followed in his mind's eye to haunt him. He let out a fierce growl slamming his open hands against a giant evergreen sending it crashing to the ground with a thunderous boom that echoed for miles through the forest. He heard the rumbling of an avalanche above him in the Alps. Vettorio pushed back the hood of his mantle. Gloved hands drawn in tight fists; he paced at vamp speed quickly wearing a path in the knee-deep snow down to the bare frozen ground.

He reasoned that it must have been fate for him to find her. Perhaps Thor or even Odin had arranged their meeting. He prayed to them both these past five thousand years, as his desire for a true mate had bore a gaping hole in his icy soul.

He had fed on local wenches in nearby towns. As the king, he had donor females and males at his disposal, but he had no desire to take any of them as his mate. Selena once had been a welcome distraction, but he had not felt the love of a woman in his heart since Lilith betrayed him with Baldassare.

What was this strange attraction held over him by that tiny wisp of a human? She had his cold heart burning hotter than any ember he had ever known in all of the millennia of his existence. Just a few mere glances at her had left him confused as to what was going on in his mind, in his heart. How could he trust such a feeling based on a few breathes in minutes? He had never second-guessed himself before, why now? He did not need this, did not want this, she is a human.

The vampire population had grown to what, he, the king considered manageable numbers. These numbers allowed them to coexist in the human realm and not risk exposure. He knew he must control their growth before it got out of hand, therefore he had proclaimed a law that limited creation to one progeny per maker. This was a law only Selena had dared to challenge. It was his law and he knew he was the one about to break it. He could not explain it, but she would be his mate, his

21

queen. It was decided. He had long grown tired of being alone, ruling without a queen at his side. His pull to her had to mean something. He believed strongly in fate and this was something he could not ignore. He made his way back through the snow, towards the church. He walked part of the way at a long human stride to allow his thoughts to sink in before flashing back to where he was sure she would still be perched on the church steps.

Althea did not hear him approach. Vettorio just appeared out of nowhere and was seated next to her on the church steps. "*Ehi*," she shuttered as she looked up at him. He was beyond handsome and had a charm about him that instantly gave her a sort of ease. Although a part of her remained guarded and she thought it best to keep him at arm's length.

"Easy *Freulien*, I mean you no harm." He held his hands up, palms out.

"Who are you? Where did you come from?" She spoke in whispered sobs between heavy breaths.

Vettorio took hold of her tiny, nearly frozen hand. He stood, bringing her to her feet along with him. She thought to resist him but quickly thought better of that idea. She was weak, freezing and had no idea when the *padre* might return and offer her refuge.

He looked her up and down, admiring. What a work of perfection he found her to be. "I am Vettorio of Bozen. Now, you shall accompany me to my castle lest you catch your death right here for the *padre* to find in the morrow." He removed his mantle wrapping it around Althea, pulling the hood over her head as he motioned for her to walk with him. "My home is near. There you will find haven, a warm fire and something to fill your belly." He was glad he had chosen to keep human servants in the castle; they would have food in the kitchen. "Now come, explain to me how it is you ended up here in Bozen, in this storm and sitting on the steps of this chapel."

Althea looked up at him from deep within the mantle's hood. He was breathtakingly handsome. Even in the dim light of the clouded moon and falling snow she could see those blue pools staring back at her from behind long wisps of hair. Heavy from wet snow, his dark locks, clung to his pale skin. A strong chin and chiseled cheekbones brought to mind a marble statue of Apollo she had seen in Rome as a child. She did as he instructed despite the sense of foreboding that her mind was screaming at her. Deep in her soul, he made her feel safe. She felt conflicted inside.

As they made their way toward the castle, she told him of her plight. The wailing winds required her to nearly shout out her words about how her father had given her into the care of Bernard, the Lombardi king. She had grown to care for him, as he had not been unkind to her. The king had sworn to be her protector, but then his wife had taken exception to Althea more so than the other ladies in waiting. Once she voiced her strong protest of Althea's presence he had thrown her out and exiled her from Marsi. She was droppedo ff at the church by the king's guard like so much refuse, forever soiled. She did not know why she felt so compelled to tell this stranger about her plight, but she was certain he would understand on some level what she had been through.

Althea could not see the gray granite walls until they were just a few feet in front of her. The amber flames of an oil torch barely shone from the barbican above the gate. She did not know why, but Vettorio's strong muscular arm guiding her against the oncoming winds had felt strangely comforting. She was saddened when he removed his hand from her back to motion for the lone guard to raise the gate allowing them entry into the bailey. The late hour along with the weather had the courtyard empty save for a fresh white blanket of snow. Inside the walls, they were sheltered somewhat from the winds. Vettorio guided her across the bailey to the entrance of the keep. A young squire opened the massive door just as they approached. The slight clanking of his spurred boots against the stone steps under the overhang of the arcade alerted the faithful servant that had been listening for the sound of his master's footfalls.

Althea pushed back the hood of the mantle from her face and took in her surroundings. She saw no other folk stirring in the main hall as they continued inside the threshold. The massive door was made of wood she had never seen. It looked like ash yet something told her it was not. She ran her fingers along the side of the door; the wood was silky smooth as opposed to the rough wood of Bernard's castle entrance. Vettorio nodded for her to keep moving. The door closed behind her with a thud that shook her from the awe trance her surroundings had drawn her into. The squire disappeared quickly down the corridor.

The stone walls of the main hall were well lit from sconces placed only a few feet apart on either wall between the most beautiful tapestries of mythological creatures, gods and goddesses. The room was opulent. She thought not even the king had such treasures. Just when she thought she had taken it all in, she looked up to see the fresco on the ceiling. There above her hung the sky in various hues of brilliant blue dappled with puffy white clouds illuminated by the firelight of the burning oil. She released a slight gasp from deep within at the sheer beauty of the artistry of it all, and wondered what had inspired him to choose such a painting to be on his ceiling. Usually one finds angels peeking out within such painted clouds. The simplicity of a bright sun shining through the clouds was a pleasant change.

Continuing her perusal of his castle, she saw hanging on the first landing of the staircase was a life-sized portrait of him. Those blue eyes were as hypnotic on the oil canvas as they were in the flesh. She thought his image was that of great power and wealth yet sad, dishearteningly so. It tore at her tender heart and urged her to save him from whatever demons were tormenting him. She wanted to reach out and touch the face on the canvas, tell him it would be different, but exactly how she was uncertain. She only knew in her heart there was something about to change for both of them, something strange and wonderful that would change their lives forever. She turned on her heels to look at him, a warm smile blooming on her lips.

"Please," he broke into her thoughts guiding her into what she presumed was his private solar. She had never seen so many books in one place before. "Continue. I wish to hear the rest of your story." He spoke in a soothing, silky tone as he helped her out of his mantle then hers. He tossed the wet cloaks over a tall black leather chair, one of a pair that flanked the massive marble fireplace.

Althea was overwhelmed by her surroundings, by Vettorio with his hypnotic eyes and light scruff of a beard. She watched in angst while he raked a hand through his wet hair pushing it back out of his eyes, away from those piercing eyes. She swallowed hard turning on her heels away from him, staring into the fire. The orange and red flames danced about while roaring to the top of the five-foot tall opening and licking at the outside edges of the surround. "I am no whore." She spoke softly, rubbing her hands up and down the length of her arms.

Vettorio picked up a large animal fur from the red velvet sofa. He shook it out. "And you shall never be treated as such." He held the fur blanket up between them. Smiling, he diverted his eyes to the floor. "You need to get out of those wet garments young Lady before you catch the fever." Filling his empty lungs with

28

her scent, he was reminded of fresh linen and rose water. Althea slipped out of her wet day dress and undergarments. When she had finished undressing he handed her the fur for her to wrap up in. She took a step away catching the blanket and wrapping it tightly around her. He picked up her wet garments, draped her pale green silk dress and under garments over an antler protruding from the wall next to the fire to dry.

He went back to the open fire and poured her a hot cup of tea from the kettle that had been hanging over the fire's edge "Drink this tea. It will help to warm you." He placed the cup in her hands before excusing himself to change out his own wet garments. "I shall be but only a moment. Please try to relax and warm yourself. There is more tea in the kettle should you desire another cup in my absence."

She nodded taking a seat on the floor in front of the fire. Clutching the blanket with one hand, Althea sipped the hot liquid. She had never tasted the sweet blend of Chinese tea. She picked up notes of cinnamon and honey that brought a gentle smile to her lips. This was indeed a treasure from the east. By the time he returned she had emptied the cup and had returned to staring at the fire.

He sat next to her, but not too close. He inquired as to whether she was warm enough. She assured him she was quite comfortable. They made small talk here and there, falling into silence at random moments. She could feel him watching her, but she dared not look at him for fear of embarrassing him at being caught staring at her. Then suddenly a wave of easiness came over both of them. They talked for hours Vettorio found himself laughing, a deep belly laugh, for the first time in many years. His laugh was like the feel of pure silk against her skin. She wanted to hear it repeatedly; she thought surely she could listen to the sound of his voice and that contagious laugh for endless hours and never tire of hearing it.

They stayed there near the fire until she drifted off to sleep against his arm. He shifted letting her head rest in his lap. Vettorio tenderly stroked her hair, watching her sleep and admiring her beauty. The urge to sink his teeth into her fully exposed silky smooth neck was growing, as was his now throbbing manhood. "No." he told himself in a low growl pushing back his natural instincts. He had other plans for her on this night and all of the nights to follow. Vettorio leaned his back against the chaise behind him watching her until the night gave rise to the sun.

He eased from under her, making sure the fur stayed over her shoulders and remained covering her, keeping her virtue intact. A footman had been sent to collect her trunk from the church so she had a fresh dress warming in front of the fire when she woke. Vettorio selected a cream velvet dress from her trunk and hung it to warm by the fire. He quietly turned a chair to face her and took a seat. He watched and waited for her to stir.

Althea began to stretch waking up. She snuggled into the soft fur smiling without opening her eyes. Part of her was afraid to open her eyes to this new day in fear that last night had been but a pleasant dream.

Vettorio cleared his throat, got up and went to collect her dress. He picked up the soft cream velvet garment folding it into a neat package and tucking it under his arm before walking to Althea and offering his hand to help her up. "My dear, let me escort you to the bath. I am sorry I did not offer you the use of it last night in my defense I was swept up in our conversation. It was pleasant to be sure; however, I should have offered my guest a warm bath in refuge against the cold winter's night. I ask that you forgive me this slight." He helped her to her feet, and then helped her adjust the fur around her shoulders. He hoped she had no doubts he had been none but a gentleman whilst she slept. Leading her out of the solar with an open hand pressed gently into her back, they walked to the end of the main keep where he opened the door to a spacious bathing area. "You will find the waters comforting." He leaned against the wall letting his right hand dance beneath the water flowing into the pool. "The ganat brings water from the hot springs of the Bagni Vecchi in Bormio. Some warmth is lost in the miles of travel but it is still quite warm and carries the healing properties of the springs." His lips bloomed into a bright smile. "Bormio is near where Apollo chose to place his temple some fourteen hundred years ago. He filled the water with its magical healing properties. Or so it has been told," an eyebrow raised as if he were skeptical of the event rather than present to bear witness to the raising of the temple. A grumble from her stomach reminded Vettorio she was human and needed to have food. "I will have Cook make you breakfast whilst you bathe *meine dame*." He looked up at the young hand maiden standing silently with her head bowed in the doorway waiting to be invited in the room. "Come in child." He instructed the young woman to see to Lady Althea's every need then left them alone, closing the door behind him.

Althea smiled brightly, "I am Althea, what is your name?"

The young girl kept her eyes averted to the floor. "They call me Sara, milady." She answered in a tiny low voice. Sara approached Althea slowly, and then took the fur from around her letting it drop to the floor.

"Have you been in Vettorio's employ very long?"

"I was birthed here in the castle milady, near six and ten years ago now," Sara replied. The young girl wondered if she was aware of exactly with whom she had come upon. She feared as much as she respected her master and would not dare to speak out of turn where he was concerned. Sara tied her skirts up at her knees and stepped onto the stone bench at the edge of the bathing pool. She held her hand out to Althea and guided her down the steps into the warm water. The younger girl sat down on the edge while Althea sank down to her shoulders in the pool. The water felt amazing. It eased the strain in her muscles that she was not aware she had, Sara immediately picked up a large sea sponge, rubbing it into a sweet scented paste held in a turquoise bowl at the water's edge. She rubbed her hand against the paste until it began to lather and then she gently began to wash Althea's neck and shoulders.

"That smells heavenly, Sara. Whatever is in there?"

Sara smiled, "The ash is mixed with the oil of olives from the south, crushed rose petals and lotus blossoms with just a bit of honey borrowed from the bees." She

34

explained as she began washing Althea's long copper tresses. Working up a thick lather then combing through her hair with a double-sided comb made from a solid piece of ivory.

Althea felt her whole body relax. The warm healing spring water caressed her skin. The fragrance of the soap was intoxicating. She felt her mind drift as she closed her eyes. Vettorio appeared in the darkness behind her eyelids. She thought him the most handsome man she had ever laid her eyes upon. His skin soft and smooth with just a touch of sun kissed color and his eyes the color of the Mediterranean Sea she had seen on a visit to Greece. He spoke with the voice of an angel. She thought how fortunate for her he had come upon her on those steps, but she feared herself unworthy of such a man as he. After Bernard, how could any man of substance ever look upon her as worthy? She felt tears begin to pool behind her closed eyes. Sara poured water over her to rinse away the soap, bringing her back to the present. When the bathing was done, Sara helped her dry off and dress in the dress Vettorio had selected. The two young women conversed like long lost sisters as Sara combed her hair then braided it.

"You are truly a rare beauty." Sara looked her up and down smiling.

"Oh," Althea said, while blushing, "I don't know about that. I don't think I am anything special but thank you for saying so."

Smiling at her, Sara asked, "Shall we?" She held the door open for Althea then walked with her to the dining room. Sara curtsied to Vettorio then went off to the kitchen humming a lullaby.

Vettorio got up from the dining room chair where he had been perched waiting for her to return from her bath. He went to her offering up his bent arm to escort her to the table. She wrapped her tiny arm around his with a warm smile and went with him. "Did you enjoy your bath?" He asked, feeling rather anxious that she may not be impressed with what he had to offer after living at the castle of the Lombardi king.

"I did indeed. It was heavenly, thank you so much again for your kindness." She smiled warmly.

"It is nothing. It pleasures me to know someone else is enjoying the amenities of this place, other than me and the servants. I've not had company…" He trailed off, pretending to think, knowing he had never had company outside of his daughters in his home. "Well it has been ages. Come now, let us eat. I trust you are hungry." He smiled softly.

Cook had prepared her a nice breakfast of fresh eggs and ham. Vettorio pushed food around on his plate taking an occasional bite, as not to be obvious that he was not really eating while he watched her enjoy her meal. He refilled her glass with milk. "This is the coldest milk I think I have ever had," she grinned.

"Cook leaves it in the snow on winter mornings after the milk maid delivers it to her." Vettorio laughed and winked at the short, chubby woman dancing about the dining room table with much more spirit than you would expect for her sixty and eight years.

"That was delicious. I enjoyed it very much." Althea smiled at cook and picked up her plate. Vettorio caught her hand and shook his head no, prompting a scowl from her before she returned the plate to the table.

"May I clear the table now, your majesty?" Cook inquired with a big grin then immediately began to clear their plates. She smiled and flashed him one of her motherly, 'I know what you're up to' looks. He returned her smile adding a wink, which gave her the giggles. She had lived at the castle since her birth. Her mother and grandmother before her had been the cook for the castle. Anastas, Cook, knew what he was and she respected more than feared him. He had been a kind and generous employer to her family for three generations. She was excited to see Althea with her king. He had never had a woman spend the night in the castle before, at least she had never known one to and she thought herself quite observant. Cook saw something strange and awe inspiring in his demeanor this day and she liked it.

Cook's words echoed in Althea's head, Your Majesty. YOUR Majesty? This beautiful castle, the fine cut of his tunic with its pearl and ruby buttons, who is this man that she had suddenly found herself besotted with? Questions whirled about in her mind sparking a range of emotions that shone clearly in her eyes, squishing her entire face, and making her bite her lower lip.

Steepling his fingers under his chin Vettorio leaned his elbows on the table. He looked on, holding back the laughter building in his belly, amused at the expressions running across Althea's face.

Althea took a deep breath and looked him in the eyes. "Why did she call you that, may I inquire?"

Crossing one knee over the other of his long legs, he brushed the back of his hand against the soft material covering his thigh. He let go the deep roaring laugh that had built up deep in his belly. "Yes, you may. As I told you, I am Vettorio. Moreover, yes, you could say I am a king of sorts; there are those that call me such. Mine is not a kingdom recognized by the Emperor. Bozen is but a small part of my kingdom. I shall explain fully at another time. But this day is not that time." He walked around to her side of the table offering his hand to her.

"It is a beautiful day. Accompany me on a sleigh ride down to the lake." He smiled softly.

She took his hand and went with him. Vettorio took care to insure she was wrapped snugly under a pile of furs in the sleigh next to him before he instructed his coachman, "Onward to Lake Garda." They rode by the lake stopping from place to place to admire the beautiful iced over pool of water that glistened a silvery blue under the sun. He watched her as she took it all in with the wonderment of a child. Viewing the scenery anew through her eyes brought him much joy. "Shall we stop here for a bit of refreshments? Cook has prepared us a basket. I think this is a lovely place to stop." He motioned to the view. They were right between the mountains where you could see far and wide. Althea was in awe of the snow covered Alps in the distance that were encircled in crowns of winters gray clouds tall in the sky. They shared breads and cheese with wine from a basket prepared by Cook.

"It is absolutely awe inspiring here. I have never seen such a place. I dare say that if I was one to be fanciful, I

40

could write a sonnet about these Alps." She smiled brightly.

"You continue to smile like that my dear and the snow may start to melt." He chuckled as she faintly nudged him and blushed lightly.

They enjoyed such outings daily for some weeks. Vettorio had decided to court her, a human game he had never understood but found himself nonetheless enjoying. He felt her relax completely with him within this time and become a true part of the castle he had never shared with anyone before her. He let her know he wished her to live there with no pressure to be his mistress. He was not a creature that had ever taken anything slowly. In fact, he had always taken what he wanted. However, for once, he felt himself truly wanting to give her the time and attention she deserved. Therefore, they shared only the chastest of tender kisses on the cheek or forehead at night before she retired to her chambers. He had never felt this way about anyone and he was a bit put off by her hold over him, but he also felt he could entrust her with his dead heart. At night, when he was certain she was sound in her slumber he would slip off to feed. He knew he could not yet tell her what he truly was, but he felt as if he was betraying her by going to others for his sustenance. He had to get past those thoughts, as he knew he must feed and she was not ready to learn the truth.

Althea quickly became loved by the castle folk and known in whispers as "the lady" they all suspected would be their future Queen. Cook was overjoyed with her company in the kitchen, her eagerness to learn how to bake bread, but even more so by the new life she had brought into the castle and her King. The happiness Vettorio was finding in Althea did not go unnoticed by anyone.

Aslaug and Judit heard that Althea had moved into the castle and become a fixture in their father's life. The two agreed it would behoove them to take an interest in this human and get to know her. Vettorio could not have been more pleased when they inquired about coming for a visit to meet his Lady. He was certain they would love her the way he did and was anxious for them to become acquainted. Althea on the other hand was terrified of meeting relatives of Vettorio's. He had explained their relationship as that of distant cousins that he had taken in and become a father figure to.

When Aslaug and Judit arrived, Althea came running to greet them with a warm embrace. They all proceeded to the solar where Vettorio stood off to the side next to the fire. Judit was instantly taken with Althea and thought her the perfect mate for her father. Aslaug was a bit more standoffish, but only because she was much more reserved in nature than either her sister or Althea. When she looked to Vettorio and he nodded with a soft smile. She joined Judit and Althea in a quiet banter about everything from the recent blizzard to the promise of a beautiful spring just around the corner. Both females befriended Althea and the three of them enjoyed many pleasant hours together over the next few weeks.

There was no favor to be found in the eldest of his vampire daughters, Selena. She was jealous and wanted nothing to do with Althea. She refused to come to meet her. However, she kept a close eye on her from a

distance, growing more and more infused with hatred.

Cook prepared a lovely meal and had a table set in front

of the fireplace at Vettorio's request in the solar, and a

vessel of wine was brought up from the cellar. Flowers

from the greenhouse were arranged to perfection and

mixed perfectly with the aroma of the food she knew

only Althea would consume. Vettorio gave her a warm

smile and a nod of approval. Cook closed the doors on

her way out, leaving the two of them alone to enjoy

their meal.

"She is not very subtle." Althea giggled lightly before

biting into a boiled potato.

"No, subtle she has never been. It is one of many

things I enjoy about her." Vettorio took great joy in

watching Althea eat.

He sat back and smiled as she took her first bite of

what he assumed was a decadent goose. Wondering

what her life had been like before she was cast out, he decided to inquire further about her life with King Bernard.

"So tell me, did Bernard not feed you these delights? Pardon my saying so, but you seem rather taken with the goose. I do not mean to pry."

Althea blushed as she wiped the corners of her mouth with her napkin. "Oh to be sure he did. However, nothing was prepared such as this. I have had goose before, but whatever cook has done with it has made it taste like none before. I must ask her how she did it." She smiled.

Chuckling, he leaned forward to move some food around on his plate and put the empty fork in his mouth. "My dear, while you are here, you will never need for anything nor need to feed anyone in this household. You should feel at home here. Not a servant."

"I know, your grace, I just do love to cook and learn as much as I can of the art of it. I have never really been able to keep my head out of the basic functioning of a

45

castle It has been a hard lesson to learn that I do not have to do it all myself. I have been truly blessed since entering the court of Bernard. Until he cast me out, that is."

"Well, you are here now and you need not worry about being cast out. You are always welcome here."

Seeing he was barely eating, Althea looked him in the eyes, with a look of embarrassment. "You have barely touched your food and I have you talking. Please, let me allow you to eat some. You have been so gracious to me and I should not be happy to know that I kept you from sustenance."

"My dear, I find I am not too hungry at the moment and besides, I do find happiness watching you enjoy what I can give you. Do not fret over me getting sustenance. I will find it when I need it. Here, let me ring for dessert. I am positive Cook can impress you even more with what she has concocted." He rang the bell sitting on the table and instantly, as if she had been standing right outside the door, cook came in with the dessert.

With dessert on the table, Vettorio leaned forward and took a spoonful of the bread pudding. "Here, let me feed you. It will allow me to experience it through you, as I am unable to eat it. It does not agree with me."

She had wondered why none was put in front of him, but did blush at the idea of him feeding her. She leaned forward and opened her mouth slightly. He placed the spoon at her lips. She moaned at the first taste, licking her lips as the sweet taste delighted her taste buds. She was glad she had not told him she did not care for bread pudding. He was correct, Cook was wicked at the concocting of food and she loved her bread pudding.

He took his time allowing her to savor each bite of the dessert until she professed she could not take another bite. He then poured them wine and they talked and laughed for hours after their meal had been consumed.

Althea was filled with a sense of inner peace she had never known in her nineteen springs. She felt as if she had been lifted by a whirlwind and caught up in a dream

47

with Vettorio, her champion dragon slayer. She giggled aloud. Her thoughts brought a pink blush to her cheeks when she noticed him staring at her.

Vettorio got up and walked around the table. Taking her hand in his, he placed a chaste kiss in her palm. She came to her feet. Facing him, she looked up into his gaze and smiled. In one fell swoop, she was in his arms. His mouth close to hers, sharing the same breath. He tenderly ran his tongue across her soft pink lips before exploring deeper into her sweet mouth that opened inviting him inside. She tasted of the sweet wine they had consumed. Moaning, he released her mouth and stared into her eyes.

"Althea, I would like nothing more than to take you to my chambers. If I am to be honest I must confess I have wanted…" he hesitated, "…you in my bed for some time. However, I didn't want to frighten you. If you see fit to come with me now you have my word the journey we embark upon will only go as far as you wish it to, and nothing will happen you do not consent to."

All she could do was place her hand in his and nod slightly. He beamed at her a smile that was more luminescent than the sun and led them to the staircase, up the stairs and past her room. She should have felt nervous, but in her heart of hearts, she knew this was right.

His master chambers were even more opulent than the beautiful room where she had slept the past weeks. The room was warm and gently lit from the fireplace. A crescent moon peeked through a small window. Vettorio placed her gently on the thick down filled mattress of his massive four-poster bed. Heavy crimson velvet drapes framed an ebony stained headboard, a grand dragon with his fiery breath and his wings spread wide were carved in great detail in the center.

His hands were cool, but the layers of fur covering the bed felt soft and welcoming under her skin. "Are you cold? I can add more logs to the fire."

"I am a bit chilled but I think it is more from nerves than anything else."

"Althea, if this is something you would rather end, let me know and I will allow you to go back to your room and hold no ill will toward you."

She reached up to his face with her hand and palmed his cheek. Looking over the planes of his face until she reached his eyes, she then focused on them and saw they were searching for an answer from hers. "Vettorio, I do not know how it is I know this is meant to be, but I do. I want to be with you in every sense. I do not want to only be taking up living space with you. I want to be a part of your life. It sounds strange to even myself, but I cannot stop this. Please forgive me for being standoffish. I am just shy, as I have never had these feelings before."

He let out a heavy sigh and rested his forehead on hers. "That is all I needed and wanted to hear."

He smiled down at her, turned and went to the fire adding several nearby logs before slowly skinning off his tunic and boots. Her eyes fixed on him walking back to the bed; she allowed them to trace his handsome form, from his perfectly chiseled jaw line to his toes. With the newly stoked fire casting a glow behind him, Althea could not help but admire his perfect muscular frame and his hardening manhood.

Climbing into the bed, he tugged the drapes together behind him, closing them inside the dark silken cocoon and shutting out the crisp air floating in through the slit window.

Althea's emotions were wrenching inside her in contradictions. She did not do such things. The Lombard king had been her only lover, but she could not deny the desire burning deep in her soul for this man. As his lips began to explore her face and neck she wanted him as she had never wanted Bernard. She ached with desire; her body quaked under his every touch.

Vettorio unlaced her bodice revealing her creamy bare skin, slowly and with more tenderness than he had thought himself capable of, and tenderly caressed her breasts. The tiny pearl peaks hardened under his fingers, goose bumps spread across her as she arched her back.

Crawling to the bottom of the bed, he removed his britches, unleashing his steely manhood. Althea let loose a small gasp. Picking up one of her legs, he placed a kiss against her ankle that he held in his hand. Easing himself between her legs, he continued kissing his way up to her smooth ivory inner thigh. His experienced tongue and fingers explored her tender folds in a way she had never even dreamed of. Bernard had never done such things. Such wonderful Earth shattering things that were sending lightning bolts through her body, causing her heart rate to rise until she feared it would pound right out of her chest. Gripping her hands around the soft animal fur, she let out a moan so feral she could not believe it had come from her.

Vettorio smiled, pleased with the result of his pleasuring her. He continued his slow journey toward his reward. He had made his way to her stomach, running the tip of his tongue around her belly button while gently rolling the tender pearls of her breasts between his fingertips. He paused for a moment resting the side of his face against her belly. He could hear her blood pumping through her veins like a waterfall gushing in his ear. Beyond that, he could hear the faintest beat of a tiny heart. He felt his lips curve into a huge smile. Without speaking, he continued his pathway of kisses until they were facing. Tracing the outline of her lips with his index finger before bringing his mouth full force against hers, their mouths crushed together in the most insatiable hunger for one another.

Pulling back from her, he looked into her eyes with a fierce look of tenderness. "After this, there is no turning back. If you need me to stop, you only have to say so and I will." Searching her eyes, he felt his mind begging her to not tell him no. He knew he would not be able to handle it. He could stop. However, his hunger for her was nearly unbearable. She was his from the moment he laid eyes on her, he felt childish in thinking so, but he knew it to be the truth, she was his and he was hers.

She shook her head and his heart that no longer beat almost crumbled to ash. However, her next words were something he would never forget. "Make me yours, Vettorio. I belong to you and I want you to belong to me. By the gods I do not understand it, but make it so."

With those words, he entered her slowly, gently increasing his pace. Her tight walls gripped his manhood. He felt her back arch and her pulse quicken. Althea knotted her fingers in his hair pulling him back for a deep kiss, their tongues dancing like woodland fairies at the back of her throat. He brought her to the edge of climax time after time. When he was sure, she was spent, in one final thrust he unleashed a feral growl deep from inside of himself that was matched by her own screams of pleasure in unison. Vettorio turned his face away. He was not ready for her to see the fire in his eyes or the fangs that had dropped at his moment of climax.

"Oh dear gods." She moaned.

Not exactly, he thought, a smile spreading across his face. He blinked back the glow in his eyes whilst running his tongue across his teeth to be sure his fangs had retracted. Sliding onto his side, Vettorio propped himself up on one elbow so he was looking down into those emerald pools that had captivated him. "You are the most exquisite creature I have ever been favored to set my eyes upon." He brushed a copper curl away from her porcelain perfect face and out of those eyes, he couldn't get enough of. He longed to get lost in those eyes. If only he could become a part of her world. It was a fleeting thought he knew was not possible.

Althea favored him with the biggest smile he had ever witnessed. Her eyes lit up as her smile spread across her whole face. By Odin, he would not give her up; he could not give her up. They were fated to be, he was sure of it.

Thor or Odin surely guided her to him to fulfill his longing for a true mate. Now here she was and with the possibility of a real family growing inside her womb that he never dared hope for.

As an original that fell from grace with Lilith and Baldassare, he had never known a human life. Having been stripped of his wings, he was cursed to roam the Earth through all eternity, never growing old or dying a natural death. Although he loved his three children, daughters of his making it had been a very long lonely existence, even with Michael's visits. Vettorio kissed her forehead as he pulled her close in his arms and he watched her drift off to a peaceful sleep.

He began to form a plan whilst she slept in his arms, his chin resting on top of her head. He was positive she was not yet aware of the child growing in her belly. Therefore, he would not speak of it until his plan was set. It would take some doing and a lot of groveling on his part but after much thought he was convinced he had developed the perfect plan to make Althea and the child his own.

Vettorio spread his fingers wide and gently let his large hand rest on the fur against her stomach. He smiled again with a glimpse of pure emotion he felt for the first time in over ten thousand years.

Vettorio had watched Althea sleep all night. The morning sun peeked through the bedroom window casting a warm glow against the crimson curls clinging like lace against her ivory skin. He brushed the hair away from her face with his long fingers. Her lips bloomed into a bright smile. Opening her eyes, she caught his gaze. "Good morning, sire."

"Yes, it seems it is, very much so." Vettorio smiled back at her, tracing her jaw line with the back of his fingers. "Did you rest well, *meine Dame?*"

"Yes, quite well, Your Grace," she whispered, catching his hand, holding his open palm against her cheek. "I thought I had dreamed you," tears pooled in the corners of her eyes.

Vettorio brushed away the tears with his thumbs. "*Nein meine Dame*, I am real and it was my bed in which you did find slumber. Is it regret that has prompted those tears?" He raised a brow.

"No, not regret. I must confess I do however; have some feelings of shame."

"Why would you ever?" Vettorio scowled.

"I am no courtesan, yet I did spend the night in your chambers. In your arms." She turned away from him.

He snuggled in behind her, wrapping an arm around her waist and kissed her bare shoulder. "My dear sweet Althea you have brought such light into my darkness by your mere presence." He nuzzled his face into her hair "I do not wish to hear you chastise yourself in such a manner ever again," he whispered low and deliberate against her ear. "You shall be shown only the greatest respect by all in this kingdom, or any other for that matter, of that you may be confident." He rested the side of his face against hers. Pulling her tighter into his embrace, he held her there in silence for some time. It was late afternoon before they made their way downstairs.

Vettorio decided it was time to have his talk with Althea. After the evening meal was finished, he walked around the table. Taking her by the hand, he spoke softly.

"Come and let us talk." He led her to the solar. Vettorio pulled one of the large winged back chairs closer to the fire motioning for her to be seated. He stood behind her chair, cupping her face in his hands slowly stroking her cheekbones with his thumbs. Gazing at the flames, he gathered his thoughts before he began to explain to her just what she had ventured into.

Althea reached up and caught his hands, locking her fingers in his. She suddenly had a sense of foreboding that sent a shiver clean through her. He cleared his throat and kissed the top of her head.

"It is true, as I have said, I am called King Vettorio of Bozen," he let go of her hands and walked around to the front of her chair. Kneeling, he laid his head in her lap placing his hands at her waist.

"I am not a king of this human realm in which we reside, but of a people that are now widespread across the land from the Carolingian dynasty in the west, to south of the Indus Valley, to the far north and east of Hadrian's Wall and beyond the Viking regions to the far northwest." He felt Althea's body stiffen then tremble slightly beneath him. He closed his eyes and for the first time ever he experienced a genuine sense of fear. He was not sure what power this human had enveloped him in, but he was certain the next words he chose might well be the most important of his long existence.

Althea pushed back the lump rising in her throat, her emotions waging war inside her. Fear, curiosity, passion, compassion, she wanted all of her questions answered, and then no she did not want to know any of his truths. She wanted to hold fast to last night when her world was as perfect as she had ever known. She squeezed her eyes tight and prayed in silence to the gods that she had the strength to deal with whatever he enlightened her to. Opening her eyes, she blew out a deep breath she had not realized she was holding. Combing her tiny fingers through his hair, down the back of his neck then around to his face, she lifted his face in her cupped hands. They both felt the tension release from her body. Her lips curved into a half smile. "Please continue." Without letting go of his cheeks, she slid from the chair to the reed-covered floor next to him.

Vettorio proceeded to tell her the complete story of his existence. He felt it imperative he leave out no detail if she were to become his queen. They sat wrapped in each other's arms. He spoke and she listened silently with an open mind, passing no judgment of him. He wept bloody tears when he told her of his past as an angel with his beloved Michael.

Althea shared his pain in her heart, comforting him as best she could. Once he had told her everything about himself, he told her about the child he felt growing inside of her and that he thought he might know of a way if she were to be in agreement for all three of them to all be a family, a real family, but he must first discuss it with Odin.

Althea smiled, nodded in agreement and kissed him tenderly as she held an open hand against her stomach. She knew with everything in her she should be afraid, should get out of there, and run away as fast as her feet would take her, yet she could not. Vettorio, vampire or not had awakened something in her that would bind them together always. In the blink of an eye, he had become her world, her life's breath, her very reason for

61

existing. It mattered not to her what consequences

might result from her union with this cursed angel.

2

A Plan is Formed

VETTORIO WAS GRANTED AN AUDIENCE WITH ODIN. They were of the light and dark, but Odin had always maintained a certain amount of favor toward Vettorio. He had after all, been the only one of the gods to vote on Vettorio's behalf before the council on his day of judgment. He had also grown to have great respect for the way the cursed angel handled the plight placed upon him.

Odin was agreeable with Vettorio's plan to make Althea his vampire queen while she was still with child and have the goddesses safeguard the pregnancy to full term so the baby would be born a unique blend of human and immortal. He would be equal parts Althea, Bernard and Vettorio. Odin would arrange a meeting for Vettorio with Nona, Goddess of Pregnancy and Libitina, Goddess of Death. Odin's grandson, Forseti, would act as mediator. Forseti, the God of Justice over all supernatural disputes would have the final say in their resolution.

Vettorio was hopeful. Libitina with her flaming red hair and sea green eyes was a vain, testy bitch at best, but if he made her a pleasing offer, he was sure she would agree to his request.

The challenge would lie in him refraining from attacking her when she tested his temper and of that, he was certain she would do. She had always taken an almost demonic pleasure in taunting him, even when he was an angel.

Nona was kind and beautiful with her long soft blonde curls that framed her sky blue eyes and ivory skin. She was always a fair and just goddess. Therefore, he was confident of her approval.

It was decided.the meeting would take place at the palace of Forseti in a fortnight.

Vettorio sent a message to Althea that he would not be returning to Bozen until after the fourteen days passed and he had his meeting.

Odin accompanied Vettorio as far as the gateway to the palace of Forseti. He nodded and motioned for Vettorio to enter. He looked respectfully to Odin before continuing to the giant gold palace doors. Opening the doors, a blinding light burned into his eyes. He blinked and rubbed his eyes for several seconds before he could regain his sight. It had been nearly a thousand years since his last visit here. Everything was just as he remembered.

Golden pillars towered for what seemed like miles before meeting the solid silver ceiling above. Vettorio allowed his eyes to roam around the long hall opening up to the throne room. Even someone of his standing was in awe of such opulence.

The three were waiting, watching him approach. Forseti was seated upon his throne. Nona stood to the left. She gave him a serene smile that calmed Vettorio. He had always thought her among the kindest and most beautiful of all the goddesses.

On Forseti's right stood Libitina. She was the first to speak. Her beauty matched the fierceness in her eyes that no other goddess possessed. "Why is it you wish this which you dare to ask of us? If you do not want the child to come to any harm, you could wait until after the birth to take the woman as your queen." Her voice was strong and demanding.

Vettorio swallowed hard and chose his words carefully as not to set her off. He dropped to one knee and bowed his head respectfully before this most poisonous of females. Under any other circumstances, he would face her head on defiantly and enjoy sparing with her. Knowing this might well be the turning point of his long existence, he instead humbled himself before her. "It is my hope the child truly be mine. To be born into the world a living breathing heir, with a heart that pumps my blood through his veins. I beg of you to allow me to be his father, not his maker." He stared at the shiny marble floor, his words deliberate and soft-spoken.

Forseti and Nona watched the exchange in silence.

Libitina drew her sword tapping it against the floor as she began circling around him. It took every ounce of restraint he possessed to continue what had become an exercise in humility. She knew this and reveled in it. Using the tip of her sword, she directed Vettorio's face upward to meet her gaze. "And should I agree to this farce—"

Vettorio interrupted, "If one were to whisper in the ear of Louis the Pious that his nephew Bernard is plotting against him, the Emperor would surely have his head by nightfall and you would have the soul of the king of the Lombardi to claim as your own. Neither you nor I would have to raise a hand to his demise." He had thought long to devise a way of offering her a sacrificial soul that might not be forbidden by Forseti.

Libitina threw her head back in a roar of wicked laughter as she sheathed her sword. "Oh my dear, King Vettorio you do know how to tempt me."

Nona spoke up. "Is Bernard of the Lombardi's not the true planter of this seed, which you wish to cultivate as your own?"

Vettorio nodded to Nona. "Those words which you speak are true, but hear me. He is also a cowardice man filled with contempt and treachery that is intent on betraying his own blood, the Emperor."

Forseti waved him off directing him to wait in the hall while they deliberated his request. Vettorio bowed respectfully and took his leave.

"Well, what have you to say sisters?" Forseti questioned.

Libitina let out a subdued laugh. "I think it was brilliant of him to come up with such an idea. I am

68

actually rather impressed. I say so be it. I am willing to forgo claiming the child in exchange for Bernard." She crossed her arms at her waist and smiled smugly.

Vettorio paced the great hall until he was called back in to hear their decision. He went to one knee and bowed his head before Forseti.

"I agree to safeguard the pregnancy to term after Althea has been made queen. We shall stay by her side at the birth to ensure the young Prince enters the world unscathed." Nona spoke softly with a slight smile on her lips. Libitina merely nodded in agreement.

Althea had been pacing nervously in the solar. The sound of Vettorio's booted footfalls were a joyous clatter that sent her running to greet him. "What did they say? Did they agree?" She flung herself into his arms, hurling her questions one after the other, "Are we going to be a family?"

He smiled widely lifting her in the air, twirling around in circles. "Yes my dear, we are to be a true family." Letting her down gently back to the floor he took her face in his hands gazing deeply into her eyes before kissing her passionately. Breaking from their kiss, he took her hands in his. Dropping a knee to the floor, he looked up longingly into her eyes. "My dearest Lady Althea, will you do me the great honor of becoming my wife, my Queen?"

Althea could not hold back the flood of tears building in her emerald pools. "There is no greater joy I could ever imagine than to be by your side forever, my beloved," she whimpered. Going to her knees in front of him, she pulled her hands free and cupped his cheeks tenderly. "Make me your true wife my beloved Vettorio and I shall spend all of my days and nights proving my devotion to you."

"You have nothing to prove to anyone," he grinned, "but should you wish to shower me with your affections, you shall find no resistance in me." He pulled her close in a warm embrace before resting his forehead to hers.

Cook had witnesses their exchange from the kitchen doorway. A stifled giggle caught his attention and Vettorio looked at her over Althea's shoulder and gave her a wink. She spun on her heels in a thunderous laugh and ran off to spread the good news.

Vettorio and Althea chose the Feast of Saint Valentine as the date for their union. Vettorio shared the story of Valentinus of Rome with her. "I did not have the pleasure of knowing him well; however I grew to have great respect for his strong convictions. Even though I offered to free him from Roman imprisonment he declined with grace and remained imprisoned for performing weddings for soldiers who had been forbidden to marry." Vettorio paused to clear the lump in his throat brought on by the memory of a man he once knew and respected. "His jailer, Asterius had a daughter that had fallen ill. Valentinus healed the girl and became rather taken with her. His farewell letter

71

written to her and signed 'Your Valentine' was his only goodbye written before he was executed."

Althea listened hanging on every word, gasping lightly as the story touched her heart. "I agree, honoring his memory with a celebration of our love would be most befitting of the occasion," she responded with a bright smile.

Aslaug and Judit joined them in the solar to plan the wedding. It would still be frigid in February so they agreed on the ceremony taking place in the greenhouse. It would be easy to turn it into a floral paradise with just a simple rearranging of things. A wondrous variety of greenery and flowers flourished under the great expanse of glass. The massive greenhouse was constructed and filled with his favorite flowers as Vettorio's reminder of a paradise where he once lived but could never return. He stood back, leaning against the doorway of the solar and watched as the three women awed and giggled at the ideas they shared. He smiled at Althea each time she looked up to catch his gaze. He had a sense of being; of belonging that he had never known before, not even when he was an angel.

Aslaug and Judit along with Cook had turned the greenhouse into a magical wonderland of botanical treasures from around the world. A bolt of white silk from the Asian province was rolled out to create a narrow isle bordered by white rose bushes and calla lilies with vessels of babies' breath, white lotus blossoms and fragrant peonies tucked in between. Two pairs of white doves were set free inside the greenhouse. They perched upon an arch covered in specific flowers in the ancient Chinese tradition to represent the four seasons; white lotus and peony for summer, osmanthus and chrysanthemum for fall, flowering plum, pine and bamboo for winter, peach blossoms, iris and magnolias finished it off with spring. It was truly magnificent.

A footman arrived with the local Vicker. The priest stood for some moments in the doorway in awe of the

73

sheer beauty of it all. Vettorio entered, a wide smile blooming across his lips as he took in the sight. "Come *Padre`*, shall we take our place?" He motioned and the priest followed him to stand under the arch.

Nona, Goddess of Pregnancy and Libitina, Goddess of Death arrived as promised. They sat on opposite sides of the isle at the back of the greenhouse. Nona exchanged smiles with Vettorio and the Vicker. Libitina gazed at them with a blank stare that gave the Vicker a shudder. The castle staff came in all decked out in their Sunday best and took their seats. Aslaug and Judit entered wearing cream velvet gowns. They carried willow baskets filled with rose petals and lotus blossoms, letting handfuls of the sweet fragranced treasures fall to the silk walkway beneath them. They made their way towards their father with Althea following behind them. Althea was breathtakingly beautiful in her gown of white silk and delicate lace. A row of pearl buttons adorned her sleeves. Her hair was artfully swept up and held by ivory pins encrusted with the finest crystals and emeralds that were matched only by the sparkle in her eyes.

For the first time in his long existence, Vettorio found himself absolutely awe struck. Althea was the most enchanting creature he had ever seen in all of the nine worlds or the magical realms beyond. He took her hand in his and turned slowly to face the Vicker. A human marriage had little meaning to him but he felt compelled to follow such traditions for her. For her, he wanted their union to be nothing less than perfect and that it was.

Althea felt butterflies fluttering in her tiny rounded belly. The Vicker spoke his words of marriage and promises. Vettorio and Althea could not break the hold each had on the other's eyes. In those moments, they forgot there was anyone else in the room, in the world. They barely noticed when the grapevine braided with the thirteen colorful ribbons symbolizing their words of commitment was wrapped around their hands binding them in the Handfasting.

Red symbolizing will, love, strength, fertility, courage, health, vigor, and passion.

Orange for encouragement, adaptability, stimulation, attraction, plenty, and kindness.

Yellow to embody attraction, charm, confidence, balance, and harmony.

Green to exemplify fertility, luck, prosperity, nurturing, beauty, health, and love.

Dark Blue to epitomize a safe journey, longevity, and strength.

Light Blue to personify tranquility, understanding, patience, and health.

Purple to signify healing, health, strength, power, and progress.

Black to mirror strength, empowerment, wisdom, vision, success, and pure love.

White to illustrate spiritual, purity, truth, peace, serenity, and devotion.

Gray to illustrate balance and neutrality.

Pink to symbolize love, unity, honor, truth, romance, and happiness.

Brown to embody healing, skills, talent, nurturing, home and the Earth.

Silver to illustrate creativity, inspiration, vision, and protection.

Gold to personify unity, longevity, prosperity, and strength.

Cook and Sara cried tears of joy as the couple were pronounced man and wife. There was tons of food and drink to be had by all. Even Libitina managed a smile or two before the night's end.

Vettorio and Althea bid good night to their guests and made their way upstairs to their chambers. He swept her up in his arms and carried her to their marriage bed. Althea looked up at him, eyes filled with desire. "Make me yours forever my beloved." She pulled her wedding gown off her shoulder tilting her head, exposing her delicate neck.

"Patience, milady," he whispered capturing her mouth in a passionate kiss. Vettorio skillfully untied her bodice helping her out of the elaborate dress without breaking their kiss. He pulled back to look in her eyes.

"Are you absolutely sure? You can have no doubts for I cannot undo what has been done once I have claimed you as my Queen. You do understand this?" His eyes were filled with longing and fear at the same time.

"I have never been more certain of anything." She placed an open hand against his cheek. "I am your wife and I desire with all that I am to be your queen, to spend all eternity by your side."

They made sweet love to each other with great care and tenderness, each pleasuring the other in kind until they were both sated. Vettorio took Althea in a tender embrace, "I love you as I have never imagined possible," he whispered against her ear before taking her tender neck into his mouth and sinking his fangs deep into her jugular draining her coppery sweet life's blood until life had left her body.

Vettorio quickly jumped into his britches, covered her delicate form with a fur blanket then flashed downstairs where Libitina and Nona had been waiting in the main hall. "It is time," he called out to the goddesses before flashing back to Althea's side. He kneeled on the floor next to the bed. Taking her hand in his, he closed his eyes and held her hand to his cheek."

The goddesses entered the room. Libitina leaned against the doorway while Nona walked around the bed to the opposite side of Vettorio. She smiled sweetly sitting down on the edge of the massive bed placing an open hand on Althea's stomach.

The three of them had remained in the room with Althea's lifeless body for forty-eight hours when Vettorio began to question his decision and doubting Libitina's word not to take Althea's soul. "You have tricked me." He backed Libitina against the wall snarling, fangs dropped, his breath hot against her face. "I must have been crazed to take you at your word you treacherous bitch."

"Vettorio stop." Nona placed a hand on his shoulder. "She will be alright, you have my word. No one has deceived you here. Come let me show you." She took him by the arm and guided him back to the bed. "Place your hand on her stomach. You can feel the child, he lives still."

He gently laid his open hand on the swell of Althea's belly. The movement he felt brought a calming sense of peace to his troubled heart.

Libitina growled at him from across the room, "We have had our differences over the millennia but I have never once broken my word. I expect an apology for your mistrust, Vettorio."

He looked over his shoulder at her. "I offer my sincere apology for doubting you. I find myself in a position unknown to me. The emotion of fear is a stranger I have never longed to meet and I know not how one deals with it." He spoke deliberately then focused his attention back to the woman he loved more than his own existence, lying helpless in their bed. For another twenty-four hours he stayed at her side, combing his fingers through her hair, wiping her brow with a cool cloth and just watching for any sign of her waking. Aslaug and Judit had come in and out. Their attempts to get their father to leave the castle to feed had fallen on deaf ears. He refused to leave Althea's side for even a few minutes insisting her blood had been enough to sustain him for some time.

It had been seventy-two hours since Vettorio had bitten her when Althea began to stir. She opened her eyes slowly to see him staring at her "Hello, my King." She smiled softly and his heart melted.

"My work is done here. I bid you farewell." Libitina nodded to Nona and Vettorio then turned and left.

Nona smiled sweetly at Althea. "I shall take my leave as well but shall return before your time comes to bring that sweet babe into the world." She touched her hand to Vettorio's arm, "All shall be well, and of that I assure you."

The next two months passed quickly. Aslaug and Judit spent much of their days with Althea. The nights of course belonged to Vettorio. He taught her to feed from him alone. It became a ritual that gave him great pleasure and an anomalous sense of purpose. The idea of his bride feeding from another was inconceivable; furthermore, he wanted only his blood coursing through her veins giving life to their baby.

They found that Althea still craved human food and much larger amounts of it than she would have ever consumer before. "It is the wee one, I am sure of it." Cook reckoned to Vettorio with a boisterous laugh

Nona returned as promised the day before labor began. No one could be certain of exactly what they should expect, as this pregnancy was the first of its kind.

Being a vampire did not lessen the pains of labor for Althea. Her labor was hard and lasted nearly twenty-four hours. Vettorio was beside himself with worry. Aslaug and Judit tried to calm him but there was no comforting him. He paced and cursed until Michael appeared next to him, arms wide open. The two of them embraced, Vettorio broke down, allowing the tears that had been building up inside of him to flow freely.

"What have I done? She is in such agony. I fear she and the child will not survive it." Vettorio sobbed.

"Women have survived the pain of childbirth since the beginning of man my friend." Michael smiled, "You have just never witnessed this amazing feat only a woman could ever bare." Michael nodded to Nona, "Greetings goddess."

On that very night was born the first living breathing heir to the Kingdom of Darkness. King Vettorio declared his son to be known as Prince Bonaventura (Bo-nah-ven-too-rah) from the Latin meaning good fortune. He had taken the winged birthmark on the baby boy's back as a sign from the gods that his son would indeed be special.

Michael wept when Vettorio placed his son in his arms asking the angel to pray for the boy. His wings unfurled fully wrapping himself and the newborn in a feathered cocoon. The angel prayed to the gods to bless Bonaventura and keep him safe. "I shall watch over you always," he added, kissing the baby on the forehead.

Therefore, it came to pass that at that same time, Bernard the First, King of the Lombardi was dethroned and blinded before dying on the order of his uncle,

Emperor Louis the Pious for treacherous acts on the 17th day of April in the year 0818 AD.

Bonaventura grew up with a relatively normal childhood, save for the fact his parents were the King and Queen of the vampires, and he had an angel as his closest friend and guardian. Two of his sisters, Aslaug and Judit showered him with affection, but the third sister, Selena shared no such love for the child. To her he was but a thief, an abomination that stole all of Vettorio's attention. She had made several failed attempts to rid herself of him since his birth. She nearly succeeded just past his tenth birthday. His guardian angel was away in Rome and Vettorio was in town. Selena watched from a distance as Bonaventura ventured off alone into the Alps. She checked to be sure Althea was nowhere in sight before following a safe distance behind him. The young boy had hiked about five miles up the mountain when the thunderous slamming of horns together caught his attention. He stopped to watch as the two large rams began their ritualistic dance of threats, aggression and submission used to prove dominance and claim their right to mate the chosen females. He stared in awe at the power thrust upon one another by the rams as they clashed horns until the younger male was forced into submission. Bonaventura was smiling at the wild goats, shaking his head when he heard someone come up behind him.

"Hello, young Prince." Selena was behind him, spun him around and pinned him against a large boulder. She let a sharp nail scrap down his cheek drawing blood. The fear in the boy's eyes gave her immense pleasure. "I am more than pleased to see you fall to your death." She licked the blood from his cheek and motioned to the edge of the nearby cliff.

Had Michael not returned and made an appearance at just that moment she would have killed Bonaventura. The angel and female vampire were caught in a fit of battle. Selena had harbored a hatred for Michael ever since he refused her sexual advances several years prior. She attacked like a rabid wolf, fangs dripping saliva, eyes blazing. His wings unfurled with a snap, white light sparking in his eyes. The boy watched in terror as the two of them slammed one another against the mountainside. The waves of energy they released echoed through the Earth resulting in an Earthquake felt for hundreds of miles.

Vettorio flashed to the scene between them, pinning Selena against the still trembling mountainside. "What is the meaning of this?" he demanded, his forearm thrust beneath Selena's chin, Michael's blood dripping from her mouth onto Vettorio's arm. She glared at him in silence. He looked over his shoulder at Michael. "Well?"

Michael picked Bonaventura up in his arms gently brushing dirty tears from the child's face. "You need to put a leash on your spawn before your son is no more." He growled walking away with the boy in his arms, his wings retracting.

Selena gritted her teeth glaring defiantly, refusing to speak. "Very well then, this is how it shall be, you may move on to a place of your choosing outside of this land. You or any of your minions are not to step foot within one hundred miles of Bozen until your brother has reached maturity and then only if he sees fit to allow you back." He released his hold on her and she flashed away. In the distance, Vettorio heard a banshee cry from Selena that resulted in an avalanche in the distance.

It was not until he turned twenty and four years and eleven months that he began to transform. Until then it was uncertain how he would be affected by his parentage. At first, Vettorio summoned Michael to come to the castle in fear his son had fallen ill and might parish. A very painful process lasted from one full moon until the next. Michael, Vettorio and Althea kept vigil at his bedside. The extreme pain pulsed through Bonaventura like lightning strikes. His body convulsed, hot with fever, and covered in a heavy sweat. His parents, with all of their power, useless to subdue the anguish engulfing their child, could only watch and pray to the gods.

Michael wept and held Bonaventura's hand refusing to leave his bedside for even a moment until the transformation was complete.

The young man awakened as a mortal man no more. He had fangs, but discovered he could survive on only occasional consumption of blood. He had a unique gift that allowed him to venture inside the mind of others. He could gently read a human's thoughts or literally set the brain a blaze of an immortal.

Michael and Bonaventura continued to spend many days together. With the angel's guidance, the young man learned to control his ability. The two of them practiced repeatedly until Bonaventura could gage how much power he needed to merely read Michael's thoughts without sending him to his knees in pain.

He fed on local forest creatures as he had distaste for the idea of feeding on humans. Although Michael found it distasteful himself he went along with Bonaventura to hunt and learn to kill his sustenance as humanely as possible. They hiked high into the Alps, making a game of the hunt. Michael taught the boy the history of the nine worlds and all of the creatures that shared it.

As the next thousand plus years passed, Michael and Bonaventura grew somewhat apart. Michael took up the cause of the Crusades and began spending more and more time either in other realms or fighting the cause of the newly developing Christian race

In his absence, the dark Prince began to frequent unsavory dens where he developed a taste for opium. It was there he met a lovely Persian girl that he took a liking to. Her name was Gulbahar and he thought her true to the meaning behind her name, like a rose in spring. She always smelled of fresh rosewater and jasmine. Her eyes and hair were the color of the blackest raven, with lips full and tender. They enjoyed a brief courtship. One sunny spring day Cook prepared him a picnic basket and he took Gulbahar down to Lake Garda. They shared a skin of sweet wine and cheese. Bonaventura pulled off a piece of roasted venison, placed it on some torn bread and fed it to her. Watching her luscious lips open and close, her tongue licking out to catch the juices from the meat in the corner of her mouth drove him to near madness. His manhood grew painfully steel hard, aching to be released from the constraints of his britches. He wiped a crumb of bread from her lip with his index finger. Gulbahar turned her head slightly catching his finger teasingly between her teeth. He came to his knees. Pulling his finger from her grip he crushed his lips to hers sending them booth down into the tall grass.

Their kisses increased in depth and passion. Untying her bodice, he slid his hand in to cup a tender breast. Her tiny pink pearl felt sublime as it hardened between his forefinger and thumb. He was quickly losing his battle for control of his natural instincts.

Before he could stop himself, he had ripped her dress free of her body and tossed it aside. She whimpered slightly beneath him when he released his manhood, sliding it between her tender folds. "I promise I won't hurt you," he moaned against her neck running his tongue from her ear to her shoulder. They rocked against the ground in unison.

She arched her back deeply, crying out with pleasure.

Her carotid artery was pulsating, he could hear her blood gushing, and smell the sweet coppery liquid. He turned his head away in an attempt to subdue his desire but the urge to sink his teeth into the creamy flesh of her neck was overpowering him. He lost all control to his vampire within. Just as he was about to spill his seed he sank his fangs deep into her neck. The pleasure this brought him and her was beyond euphoric He pulled the warm nectar from her willing neck growling low, it rolled slowly down the back of his throat. It was his first taste of human blood as well as his first taste of sex. He wondered how he had gone so long without either of these pleasures, but he knew instantly that it was the first of many times to come.

He quickly discovered, much to the satisfaction of his delighted partners, even among the vampire population he had an unmatched sexual prowess. Feeding on his sexual partners at the moment of his release sent the young women into a crazed state that had become almost an addiction for him, as was his visits to the opium dens.

Upon his return, the angel could not dissuade Bonaventura from his newfound habits of ill nor could he condone them. He could no longer stand aside and watch Bonaventura fall more and more deeply into the thralls of lust. He knew he must try to reach him once more, but in the back of his mind, knew it would not work. He was Vettorio's son after all and that vampire had a stubborn streak in him that went back ages. "Listen to me and hear my words clearly. This life you are carving out for yourself can lead to no good Bonaventura." Michael pleaded.

Bonaventura was in an opium fog and did not care to hear the angel preach at him "Leave me be, it's not like any kind of overindulgence could kill me," he smirked shoving Michael away.

Bonaventura continued to frequent dens of ill repute for several centuries until he became bored with the drugs and orgies.

Michael's visits came less and less frequently until suddenly without any explanation he never returned after a trip to Rome in 1999.

Both Vettorio and Bonaventura searched the corners of the Earth and all the other realms for him and grieved terribly when they concluded he must have met death. Vettorio nearly cried a river of bloody tears. Many were brought before him to be questioned for over a year and more than a few of Selena's minions were put to death at the hand of Vettorio himself. He was convinced that someone knew what had become of his brother and he wanted answers.

Bonaventura wept in solitude high in the Alps where he had spent so many happy hours with Michael. For five years he thought of little else, he felt like his very

soul, as dark as it might be had been ripped from

within.

3

Michael's Heart Weighs Heavy

THE GERMAN PEASANTS' WAR WAS EUROPE'S LARGEST AND MOST WIDESPREAD POPULAR UPRISING, to date. Michael had received word there was a plan to put an end to this battle in Frankenhausen. He felt compelled to intervene and save as many souls as possible. Making his way to the battlefield, arriving just before dusk on May 15, 1525, he was too late. Thousands of peasants lay slaughtered in every direction. The sight of such carnage sickened him beyond compare. Weeping, he walked among the dead and dying offering comfort where he could.

Seeking council for his heavy heart, Michael traveled to Asgar to visit the gods. He walked around Gladsheim conversing with Odin. "Father, I fear the weight of my heart has grown beyond my capacity to carry it. The atrocities I have witnessed on Earth have just become too much for me to bear." His words were sullen and his eyes filled with angst.

"Tell me, if this is such a burden then why do you choose to walk so closely among the human race?" Odin questioned as they walked out of the massive golden doors into the garden. "You have a place here by my side, should you so choose."

"I have grown rather fond of mankind over the millennia." Michael looked at Odin, eyes filled with questioning anguish. "I do not understand why…" he hesitated looking down at the ground, "…why do you allow such things to befall man?"

Odin placed a massive open hand on Michael's shoulder. "Whatever becomes of the human race is their own doing for it is they that have turned a deaf ear to the gods. The faithful are few and far between." Odin motioned for him to take a seat on a nearby bench beneath a giant ash. Sitting down next to Michael he continued, "You have always been the most compassionate among the archangels and it sorrows me to see you in such pain, my son. I sense there is more behind the sorrow I see in your eyes. Share with me all that weighs heavy on your heart."

Michael looked up into the eyes of the All Father. "In recent centuries, I have found my influence over Bonaventura has waned to nearly non existent. Despite many attempts to dissuade him from an illicit lifestyle, he continues to indulge in a multitude of exotic mind-altering substances and sexual escapades. Being immortal may save him from death, but I fear for his humanity," he shook his head in despair.

"You have been there for the boy since his birth. Had it not been for you, he would surely have perished before reaching maturity." Odin raised a brow. "Selena would surely have ended him, from what I have been informed."

"Selena is yet another stone weighing me down. In all of time, I had never known loathing in my heart until the day I witnessed her with her bony fingers wrapped about that child's throat." Tears began to well up in his eyes. "I still taste the bitterness of that animosity on my tongue." He leaned forward washing his hands down his face. "How could I possibly redeem myself after harboring such hatred inside of me for centuries? I have failed to rid myself of this darkness no matter the effort I have put forth."

Odin felt his own heart sink in empathy. "My beloved angel, you were among the first in creation," he waved his hand toward the stars that twinkled in the distance above the Earth, "you were born before those stars were hung. You have witnessed the evolution of humankind, their countless atrocities, plagues and wars against one another. The council has found few redeeming virtues in man yet you have given them nothing but compassion and grace when they deserve only wrath. I would gladly grant you absolution, but it is within your own heart you must exonerate yourself. If ever there is anything I can do to give you peace, do not hesitate to seek me out and it shall be granted."

But what kind of solace would it be? Michael could not help but wonder if there would ever be peace for him. He felt he let down the very man and child he held closest to his heart, had let down the humans he felt to protect. Odin was correct. Why did he hold the humans with such compassion? They have wrought most of what they have been given unto themselves. He felt most of them were just lost and needed direction. Direction he felt compelled to give them. He stayed in Odin's presence for what seemed like an eternity. Neither of them spoke. There was nothing more for either of them to say. It was comforting to be in his company and gave him an inkling of the peace he knew he required and more time to decide what he wanted and truly needed.

He thanked Odin for the offer of absolution and told him he would ponder it and if he decided upon anything, he would alert him. With that, Michael

vanished from Odin's sight.

May 1999

Michael had gone to Milan, Italy to authenticate an

eighth-century Greek wine vessel for Vettorio. He was

about to leave the antique shop when she caught his eye.

Standing near the storefront glass, dust motes dancing

in the streak of sunlight beaming against her flawless

skin, stood a dark haired beauty whose very soul

whispered his name. She looked up from the Louis IV

chair she was admiring and gave him a slow smile. He

was perplexed by the pull he felt toward her that gave

him a sense of peace he had not felt in a millennium.

"*Buon pomeriggio signorina*," he spoke softly

approaching her. "May I be of some assistance?"

"Good afternoon to you, as well," she nodded.

"Thank you. I do have a question if I may ask? Do you

ship to the United States? New York to be exact."

"We ship worldwide," he answered tilting his head slightly taking in her petite form he towered over. She did not seem the least bit intimidated by his stature, which made him smirk and admire her even more.

"I would like to take a few pictures to send to my client. I'm an interior designer and I think this piece is perfect for a project I'm working on. If my client is agreeable, I would need you to arrange shipping for me. If it's not too much bother."

"It would be my pleasure." He instantly decided he would not be leaving Milan as planned. "My name is Michael, by the way." He grinned holding his open hand out to her, palm up.

She placed her tiny hand on his, returning his smile, "I'm Maria. It's a pleasure to make your acquaintance, Michael."

The touch of her delicate skin against his radiated the most intense sensation through his body, giving rise to a slight gasp from the angel. Kissing the back of her hand, he asked, "Could I perhaps entice you to join me for dinner whilst you wait for a decision from your client?" In his mind he was begging her not to decline. *Please say yes.*

Maria was not in the habit of taking up with strangers, but there was something she found irresistible about this man and she was sure he could be trusted. "I'd be delighted to have dinner with you."

She took her pictures and sent them from her cell phone. Michael told her about an outdoor trattoria in the canal district that served the best panettone year round. "I must confess to having an incorrigible sweet tooth," he smiled.

They decided to walk to the restaurant to enjoy the lovely spring weather and view of the canal. They chatted easily and laughed on the walk to the restaurant. He eventually had the nerve to take her arm in his and it felt just right. She fit him perfectly. She looked up to him and gave him the warmest smile he had ever felt. Warmer than even sitting in the brightest sun directly. He told her about the buildings they were passing and the short history about them. He felt like gloating, but he also knew he did not want to come on too strongly.

She admitted she traveled many places in her career; however, she never had time to spend being a tourist. She enjoyed the fact she was taking time to see the sights.

It was still early when they were seated at a table on the terrace, giving them the outdoor space almost entirely to themselves. Michael ordered an appetizer of fruit, prosciutto and Brunet cheese, espressos and a bottle of Prosecco.

"This cheese is unbelievable." Her eyes grew wider with every bite she savored.

"It is a fine goat cheese and one of my favorites." He smiled watching her enjoy the flavor. "The soft fluffy exterior opens up to a bit of attitude with its lemony tang and earthy edge. Here try this," he tore off a piece of fresh bread, smeared it with the cheese and topped it with a slice of the prosciutto before holding it to her mouth.

Maria placed her hand to his and took a bite. He watched in awe, this woman that in an instant had captured him heart and soul. Michael felt as if fireworks were exploding inside of him with this strange range of emotions that were overtaking him.

"I would never have tasted anything so divine had I not stumbled into your store. I have enjoyed this time today. I must admit though, it was mostly the guide that has made it amazing. Your flare for description is astonishing. I would never have been able to describe that cheese in such a way. Michael, you have a gift of speech I feel is of a dying breed. I have always loved the way of old speech. Mostly, I have enjoyed listening to it fall from your lips."

They both blushed and chuckled at her words. He never had anyone speak to him in this manner. He felt elated that she loved his true nature. He did not feel as if he had to modernize himself around her.

The two of them enjoyed each other's company exchanging glances and small talk about antiques and interior design until the sun had long given way to a crescent moon.

Afterward, they took a boat ride on the Canal Naviglio. Michael pointed out the sights: the Milan

Cathedral, the artist's studios, flea market, and pubs. They were gifted with the music coming from an outdoor concert. Maria had never felt such a sense of belonging as she did when Michael wrapped his jacket, along with his arm, around her shoulders. She almost floated back to her hotel as the sun was rising and Michael walked by her side. She did not want this to end and felt she must find a way to extend her time here, with Michael.

Days in fact turned into weeks in what seemed like the blink of an eye. The flea market was a daily adventure. Boat rides on the canal after dinner, had become an almost ritual for them, just before sunset every evening. Maria laughed at all of his lame jokes. Her laugh was loud and contagious, spreading to anyone within hearing distance. Michael was in awe of her almost magical ability to make strangers stop and smile watching them. It seemed as if the world around them was being drawn in to watch their love grow from a tiny sprout into a mighty oak. As much as they loved their time together, they were both new to this kind of love and were a bit nervous about voicing what was going on. It was as if they were both superstitious and did not want to break the spell they were both under. What they did not realize is that the other felt the same and there was no turning back.

Their first kiss could not have been more magical. They were on a gondola, slowly making their way through the canal. Her head was in the spot where it always was, his shoulder. She felt his tension and it bled over into her, but she refused to let it ruin the night. If there was something he needed to tell her, he would. Michael wanted the night to be perfect. He brought her favorite dessert in a picnic basket and a bottle of champagne. He knew there was a celebration going on in the village that night. Something he hoped Maria did not know about. At least to the extent of what they did to celebrate. He wanted her to think he arranged it all himself. He knew it was silly, but he wanted her to think he hung the stars themselves, just for her. Turning to her, he looked into her eyes and told her he had enjoyed the time they'd spent together more than he could ever put into words. As she smiled, he took her face in his hand and leaned in to kiss her. At that same moment, fireworks went off in the sky and she drew in a bigger breath while they were still kissing. She pulled away; they held each other and watched the show in the sky. They both felt like it couldn't have happened any more perfectly than it did. She looked back at him and they kissed sweetly again. All was right in their world.

Michael received confirmation the chair had been delivered safely to Maria's client in New York. Maria was hard pressed to return to her business and family in New York. Maria was trying to think of ways she could continue her work from Milan. She didn't want to leave Michael. She felt if she did, more than a part of her would be left behind. She never believed in love at first sight, but she was certain it was real this time. Maria reached out to all her clients to check on them, make sure there was not anything more she could do here in Milan.

It was with the heaviest heart she had ever experienced, she had to tell Michael it was time for her to go home. She could no longer do business remotely. She went to meet him for dinner, as per their usual agreement. They sat out on the veranda and enjoyed the lovely meal.

Michael could tell Maria was keeping something from him. He felt her bone crushing grief and her hesitation at speaking with him. He took her hand and gently began to rub his thumb over the top of it. "My dear you can speak to me. I know there is something weighing on you. It saddens me you feel like you cannot tell me what is ailing you." She held her head down and Michael could see a tear had fallen down her cheek. His throat seized and he could barely form words. She had found another. He would have to be a man about this and not show how much this was going to destroy him. Reaching forward with a shaking hand, he wiped away her tear. "My love, tell me please. You have me very worried. Is there something wrong with your family?"

She looked up at him meekly and took a deep breath. "No. They're all well. I'm sad because I have stayed in Milan for as long as I can. I tried to find more work for me here with my clients, but it has come time for me to go home. I'm no longer needed here."

Michael's world rocked on its axis. He heard her words. He knew he could go with her anywhere she went. He had no ties. The only tie he wanted to have was to her. But he was not going to look desperate and offer this information. It would have to be on her terms. He knew that much about her.

With a sob she went on, "I cannot imagine my life without you. I feel like I must have you in my life. I know that sounds crazy, in fact, I am waiting for the hysterical laughter to start. You cannot possibly want to follow me to New York like a puppy dog. It isn't like you to do that. Let alone the fact you have a business here yourself."

Michael couldn't bear the idea of being separated from her and was ecstatic when she mentioned him joining her. He tried to not act like the eager puppy she mentioned and not climb over the table to take her in his arms. "Maria, my love, all you have to do is ask. I would follow you wherever you asked me to. I do not understand this love we have. But I daresay it is love. You know it and I know it. I cannot give you up. I will not. I will go with you to New York and live a life with you. Do not worry about my business here. I can find someone to run it and sell what I need in order to make the move." Looking into her eyes, while holding both her hands, "I will go with you to New York, if you want me to."

Happy tears ran down her face as he explained his feelings for her to perfection. She never thought of herself as someone who needed or wanted to hear those words. She leaned forward to grab him for a kiss. In between innocent pecks, she told him she wanted nothing more than for him to come home with her. The smiles on their faces told everyone how giddy in love they were with each other.

Starting immediately, Michael sold a substantial portion of his personal antique pieces at auction. He had never really had any use for money before but knew it would be required to start a life, a normal life resembling that of a human, with Maria. While he was busy selling his pieces, she made the arrangements for them to fly to New York. She called her family and told them the news. They, of course, were a bit shocked this was something that was really going to happen. Maria was not the fly by the seat of your pants kind of girl and it made them wonder who this man was that had totally changed their loved one.

4

Life in New York

THEY FLEW BACK TO NEW YORK TOGETHER ARRIVING AT JOHN F. KENNEDY INTERNATIONAL AIRPORT. Before flying to Italy, Maria had left her car at the airport. After picking it up, she dropped Michael off at The Tribeca Grand Hotel where he checked into a suite, while she went to check in with her parents and younger brother, Nicholas at their home in little Italy.

Michael put his things away, took a shower, and then arranged for a special dinner to be delivered to his suite. He got the location of a reputable jeweler from the concierge. It was within walking distance, so Michael set off whistling on his way. It took him only minutes to decide on a one carat, marquise cut, solitaire flanked by alternating sapphire and diamond baguettes in a vintage platinum setting with a matching wedding band made of alternating sapphire and diamond baguettes. He felt confident in his choice. It was elegant but simplistic enough for Maria's modest taste. He could hardly believe how nervous he was. With every step back toward his hotel, his anxiety grew stronger. *What if I have misread her feelings? Maybe she has not even considered a future together.*

The weeks with Maria had been surreal. It was the first time in all of his millennia of existence he felt such a strong physical attraction. There had been a few women he found considerably attractive, which had stirred a certain amount of curiosity about human sexuality in him. However, it was never more than a passing thought until Maria. When he looked at her, there was something inside him that kicked his senses

113

into overdrive. Every time he kissed her, his palms became sweaty and he could feel his wings twitch beneath the surface of the skin that hid them from the world. By the time he got back to his room, his brow was covered in sweat. He busied himself making sure everything was just right. The meal was delivered: lasagna, Caesar salad, a loaf of Italian bread, and a bottle of Cristal.

Maria arrived promptly at seven.

When they looked at each other, all they could do was smile like a couple of high school kids with crushes. His brain finally registered that she was standing in the hallway and he invited her in. As she walked by, he could smell her natural scent. He loved that about her. She was so elaborate in her work, yet very simple as a woman. She did not need perfumes and he was very glad she never used any. Her natural scent was enough to hit him in the center of his gut every time she was around.

He found himself at a lack for words, which was so unlike him but he noticed she was nervous, as well. "Maria? Are things well?"

She turned to look at him with that brilliant smile and said, "Yes, I'm just very nervous for some reason." She let out a nervous laugh and he chuckled along with her. "Oh and after the grilling I got from my family, there's no way you will be getting out of dinner at their place tomorrow night. I am sorry. I tried, but my parents are very old fashioned and want to know who has stolen their daughter's heart. Then you have my brother. He may be younger, but he *is* the typical Italian brother." Smiling and laughing softly, "I almost feel sorry for you, but I never see you sweat, so it might be interesting."

His stunned looked told her he must not have thought about the family wanting to meet him promptly. She knew he had no family to speak of, so it made sense. But she would be there the whole time and no one was going to scare her man away.

"I am glad I am not the only one nervous then. As for your family? I have dealt with many a difficult client. I cannot imagine they could be worse. May I please be so presumptuous as to ask you for a hello kiss?"

She nodded her head and seemed to melt into his arms as he kissed her sweetly and softly. He pulled away and again, they both had matching smiles.

Turning to the table as he took her hand, "I hope you like what I ordered for dinner. It is nothing like what we had in Italy, but it looks appetizing." He smiled pulling out a chair for her to sit.

They enjoyed their meal over small talk and tender glances. After dinner they watched "City of Angels" at Maria's request. Michael could hardly sit still, thinking not only about the rings in his pocket but the irony of the subject matter they were watching. His thoughts bounced back and forth between the movie and his impending proposal. *Oh geez it does not work like that, not at all. Only Odin himself, well maybe Thor could grant such a request to fall. Please do not let her say no, by the gods I do not think I could bear it. I hope her father does not see this as an insult for not asking his permission first, but I must. I cannot wait another moment.*

Finally, the movie was over. He took a deep cleansing breath blowing it back out much harder than he intended. Maria gave him a puzzled look, "Are you okay?" She touched her hand to his face tenderly.

"That is yet to be determined." Michael slid off the sofa on to his knees. Turning to Maria he took her by the hand and swallowed hard. "Maria I know we have not been together very long but I love you and feel in my heart you were born to be my forever. Will you do me the honor of becoming my wife?" He pulled the ring case from his pocket popping it open in front of her.

Maria gasped, her eyes filling with tears as she held her hand out for him to put the ring on her finger. "I love you, too. I can think of nothing in this world that would please me more than to be your wife."

He placed the ring on her finger before grabbing her in a warm embrace kissing her passionately. They held tightly to one another, kissing. Michael wanted her as he had never wanted anyone before. For the first time in his long existence, he felt his pulse beating inside his growing erection. Their desire for one another was nearly overwhelming. It was difficult for Michael to pull away but he did.

Cupping her face in his hands, he looked deep into her eyes with a heated passion. "You do not think your father would feel I did him a disservice by not asking him first? I would hate to start out on the wrong foot with your family. I know how much they mean to you."

She assured him it would be something she could handle.

They kissed passionately and found themselves with him on top of her on the couch and their hands roaming all over each other. It was crazy to think he could stop, but knew he must. "I think it may be time to say goodnight my love, before I am no longer able to hold control over myself."

Maria giggled at the statement.

They straightened their clothing and he escorted her down stairs and to her car. When the elevator came to a stop, they kissed briefly, yet passionately. On a groan, she tore herself from him and walked down the hall with him following closely behind her, his open hand pressed lightly to the small of her back. She glanced over her shoulder at him every so often and found him watching her with a smirk on his face. Fanning herself, she knew she had to get herself under control before she hit the lobby and everyone would know exactly what she had been up to.

With joy in his heart and a light in his eyes Michael went to speak to Odin to request, to beg him if necessary, to grant his wish to become a fallen, a human. Once he had the confirmation from Maria and the ring on her finger, he knew this was his moment to call on a long ago promise. "You once told me should ever I come to you for a request, it would be granted. I have found my absolution Father and I wish to live out a normal human existence." His voice was low and humble.

Odin took a seat on his throne, his wolves Geri and Freki came running and sat down at his feet. He reached down and rubbed Freki's head. Looking harshly at Michael for a moment before softening his gaze he began to speak, "I did give my word to grant you any request but I must say this is unexpected. Michael. Do you fully understand the ramifications of what you are asking?"

"I do Father. I have met someone who has filled my hollow heart with joy. I want to live out a normal life, to grow old with her," he smiled respectfully.

"She must be an extraordinary woman indeed. If you are certain you wish to do that which has never been undone then I will grant this. You will be required to stand before the twelve seats of the Aesir, the council of the gods. They will vote in agreement with me and your request shall come to fruition. You have my word on this." Odin stood, embraced Michael, and then they went back inside.

Odin had mentally called the council to come together and they were seated before him in just moments. The gods being what they are, full of conceit, went through the whole procession. They listened to Odin as he made his case for Michal. They spent their time but as he promised they did agree to Michael's request.

He was instructed to go to the world tree, Yggdrasil and there as night fell so did the archangel. Michael was struck with a long series of excruciating pains that sent him to the ground and into a fetal position with his arms wrapped around his legs just under his knees in agony. He could smell his skin burning while what appeared to be a miniature-lightening bolt etched a tattoo of wings on his back. He felt as if his skull was going to explode and his back was going to spilt open. He screamed in pure torment and felt as if a century had already gone by before one last blast of misery hit him. Once the pain eased Michael was left lying beneath the tree were all life began. The once ethereal being now a vulnerable man subject to the pain and sorrow, as well as the joy connected with a mortal human existence.

Odin had been watching in the distance and waiting for the transformation to be completed. He personally returned Michael to Earth with a warm embrace and a smile. He bid him farewell.

Michael was not sure what happened and how he'd returned to his hotel bed, but he was not going to ask too many questions at the moment. He had a blazing migraine and he could hear his cell phone ringing. Or at least he thought it was his cell phone. He really had no sense of reality. He fell into an abyss of darkness and remained there for what only felt like minutes. It had been days when he finally came to. Maria was sitting in a chair in the corner, watching him.

When he looked at her, she jumped up; dropping the magazine she was holding for appearances and came to his side. He then realized he was hooked up to machines and had IVs in his arms. "My love you have come back to me." She said in a rush. "The doctors don't know what's wrong with you but knew you had to be held for observation. I'm so sorry it took me so long to find you. I feel like I could have lost you." She started sobbing on him, he put one hand on her head and petted her weakly.

"Maria," he said in a rough voice," I am well. Thank you. I would not be here if not for you. More than you will ever know."

As soon as Michael was released and cleared of all abnormalities, the wedding planning went on full force. Michael knew he couldn't wait any longer to marry the woman of his existence, his soul mate. Thankfully, Maria did not want much so it took little time to prepare. She just wanted to be married to the man of her dreams. Her parents wanted more. She was the only daughter of an Italian family, but they respected her wishes and could not be happier in the man that had stolen her heart. There was never a moment in which Michael felt like he was an outsider. From the moment he arrived at their house with a bottle of wine and told them his life's story, or at least the story he had used for many years, they opened their arms to him and made him feel like every decision he made was the best decision ever.

Maria and Michael were married in a small but elegant ceremony with close friends and family in attendance. He could not help but wish Vettorio and Bonaventura were there at his side but knew it was for the best. They left straight from the reception for their honeymoon on the island of Saint Croix. They were uncharacteristically quiet on the flight and the cab ride to their hotel, just holding hands and exchanging tender glances. Both of them were virgins and awkwardly nervous about their wedding night. Michael, one of the oldest beings ever to exist felt like a schoolboy full of performance anxiety and excitement.

The honeymoon suite was tastefully decorated. The fragrance of fresh flowers filled the air. A bottle of champagne on ice was sitting on a table, along with a dish of strawberries and chocolate that had been prearranged by Michael. He helped Maria put away their things then opened the champagne, pouring them each a glass. "Missus DeLuca you look absolutely ravishing."

Maria took the fine crystal flute in her hand smiling sweetly, "Why thank you Mister DeLuca." She took a sip of the champagne before setting the glass down on the table. "Have I told you just how happy I am that I wandered into your shop?" She leaned into him snaking her arms around his waist, resting her head against his chest.

Michael held her tightly smiling. "Not nearly as happy as I am, my love. It was my luckiest day that led to happiness, the likes of which I had never even imagined."

"You always know just what to say to make me swoon." She tilted her head back inviting his kiss and he did not disappoint. Michael took her head gently in his strong hands crushing his lips to hers in a deep passionate kiss. Maria moaned into the kiss, "I love you."

"You are love pure and simple, milady," he spoke in a whisper, pulling back just enough to lock into her eyes with his stare for several moments. He kissed her again before picking her up and carrying her to the bed without breaking the kiss. Trying to kick his shoes off in a suave manner, Michael tumbled onto the bed awkwardly on top of her prompting a giggle from Maria. They shared a laugh over the clumsiness of their inexperience.

A calm quiet settled over both of them. Michael began kissing her from her forehead down her neck as he unbuttoned her dress. Sliding the dress over her head he tossed it to the floor, and then removed his shirt with her help. Their kissing started tender and delicately but grew to a fierce passionate fencing match between two hungry tongues. He gently worked one knee between her legs parting them just enough for him to gingerly slip his body into place. Hungry lips refused to part from one another, their kiss long unbroken. Maria's breast cupped in Michael's hand was warm and delicate, her tiny pearl like nipple hardened between his fingers.

Panting, he stopped and rested his forehead on hers. "I hope I do not disappoint you. I love you so much and

126

I want to make you happy in every way. But as you know, we are both new to this. Please tell me if I do anything wrong or hurt you."

She closed her eyes and caressed his face, "You could never disappoint me. My love for you makes everything perfect. I am ready, Michael."

She gasped deeply as Michael entered between her delicate folds to claim his paradise found within her moist hot walls. They hugged his shaft, wrapping him tighter and tighter in the cocoon of her womanhood until he thought he would implode from the pleasure.

It was in one forward movement and a loud cry his seed spilled inside of her. Rising up on his elbows, he looked down into her face where he saw tears trailing out of the corners of her eyes. "Maria, my love did I hurt you? Are you alright?" He brushed the tears away with his thumb. Kissing her nose, he spoke softly, "I am so sorry."

"It's fine. The tears are from joy, my husband, well mostly. It hurt but a moment, I promise." She gave him a look filled with so much love he felt tears begin to pool in his own eyes.

Knowing she was okay, he started to chuckle, "Now *I* must apologize, for I feel like that should have lasted longer than it did. I let you down on your first time. I will have to make it up to you." Wagging his brows, he leaned down to kiss her again and was already prepared to make love to his wife again. By the time they were ready to go home, they had not seen much of the island, but had become so well in tuned to each other's bodies.

After they returned to New York, Michael decided to follow in the footsteps of his father-in-law and Maria's grandfather and he enrolled in the police academy. They did not need the money, he had plenty from the sale of his antiques, but he wanted to fit into his new human existence. Making a living like a common person was the best way he knew how.

They were truly happy, the storybook kind of happiness one dreams of. Their love grew more each day. Maria and Michael were the perfect couple that all their friends strived to be and some envied.

After five years of marriage, Michael got the biggest shock he could imagine when Maria announced she was pregnant. It was something they only briefly spoke about and the happiness of the announcement shocked him to his core. Maria mistook his shock as him not wanting the child and she burst into tears and then into a rage. He bolted from his frozen stance, grabbed her, and kissed her soundly to stop her ranting.

He then knelt in front of her, pulled her shirt up and kissed her flat stomach. "I will protect you for all of my life. You will never want for anything and you will be so loved." He cried tears he never thought he would cry. He was to be a father.

The birth of their daughter, Isabella was the most welcome gift from the gods. Michael sent many prayers of thanks daily for all he had been blessed with. She was the perfect blend of the two of them. She had him wrapped around her little finger from the moment she took her first breath. His life was now complete. Nothing else was needed for him to be the happiest man alive.

The worst thing imaginable came to be. On New Years day 2007, Maria got a call from one of her favorite clients in the Hamptons and set out to pay her a courtesy call. She was just a few miles from her destination, when a drunk driver sped through a traffic light striking her car and killing her instantly. Michael was devastated. He wept for days on end and cursed the gods above for allowing this tragedy that took away his heart and soul. His emptiness from her loss was filled with bitter hatred.

He had been unable to take care of Isabella for weeks since the funeral. Maria's brother Nicholas showed up at the door with Isabella in his arms. "Damn it man you can't go on like this. Your daughter needs you and you need her even more."

"I could not keep Maria safe, how am I to keep Isabella safe? I know nothing about taking care of a child, let alone making sure she grows up healthy and smart. Hell, I am not the smartest man in the world. Maria was Isabella's saving grace when it came to brains and beauty." He was becoming hysterical.

Nicholas shook his head with a smile on his face. "Bro, you can do this. I know you can. Maria would want you to. Don't let her down."

At first Michael turned away. He could not tell Nicholas about his fear that it was his fault Maria was taken, and if he clung to her Isabella may be taken, too. How dare he think he could just walk away, become human with no consequence? He felt like there was an act of retribution in play because of his selfish request.

Isabella cooed and said "Da." And Michael's heart melted. Nicholas put her in his arms and walked away not giving him a chance to give her back. The tiny baby girl latched on to her daddy's nose smiling and laughing like she was the funniest girl around. He knew in that moment they would be all right.

Six months later, he made the decision to move away from the city. They chose a small, southern, seaside town at random on the map and made the move to South Carolina. It was hard to leave Maria's family, but he knew if he ever needed them, they were not that far away and would be on the next plane.

Nicholas was right. He could not let Maria down. He knew she was looking down on them and was counting on him to raise their little girl. Therefore, a new start where he would not be reminded every moment about his other half missing was what they needed.

5

December 2013

Beaufort, SC

IT WAS THE SICKENING SWEET SMELL OF **STALE BOOZE,** strong perfume and the stench of death mingling with her usual Sunday morning hangover, which sent Crystal running to find the toilet as soon as she entered the apartment.

"Did you have too much Jack last night Princess?" Franco teased as he leaned down pulling her fiery tresses back in one hand and holding out a wet paper towel in the other. "I told you not to woof those sweet buns down like a lumberjack."

"It was tequila; asshole and I ate one mother freaking cheese Danish on the way here." She snatched the wet towel, wiping her face as she nudged him away coming to her feet.

"Maybe so, but that one bun was the size of that swelled up head you are carrying this morning, *mio caro*." Franco held his hands up figuratively describing how enlarged her head must feel, and then he giggled that sweet sexy little giggle that made Crystal cringe with desire.

Sarge had told her, "*You don't shit where you eat, daughter or you'll end up chewing on a turd.*" Daddy never steered her wrong so she took it to heart. Besides, she did not think Franco had ever fully recovered from his wife's death, so no matter how often she had the urge to jump his bones; she always reminded herself he was off limits.

She quickly barked out a retort, "Michael Francis DeLuca," her eyes blazing, growling at him through gritted teeth. She looked up at him from her petite stature, pulling a clip from her pocket to secure her hair up away from her face.

Smirking with a brow arched he raised his hands in the air. "Ouch, I feel it coming. You call my name as if you are my *madre* just before you slug me or tell me to piss off. Which is it *mio caro*?" Franco inquired, bracing himself for her assault.

"You know it really, really pisses me off when I don't know what the hell you're saying." She punched him in the gut, struggling to keep a straight face with him looking so lickable in those tight jeans and a white tee, grinning down at her.

"*Madre* means mother. *Mio caro*, my dear. One would think after five years working together you would have picked up a little something." He whispered in her ear as she pushed past him and headed back toward the dead body lying naked in the middle of the living room floor. He followed mockingly.

A uniformed deputy had walked the man's neighbor out into the hall to question her, out of sight of the body. A second deputy was on the phone with the sheriff.

Franco intentionally popped the rubber gloves against his wrists as he put them on before picking up a pair of pants from the floor to see if they contained any kind of identification.

Crystal followed suit. She riffled through the white cotton shirt lying on the sofa before using it to cover what she could of the naked body. "Shit, shit, shit," kneeling next to the body she gently moved the young man's head to the side. "Look at this shit," she motioned for Franco to check out the puncture wounds and red lipstick left on the man's jugular. "It's just like that kid over on Bay Street last week."

Franco squatted down on his haunches next to Crystal. He let his fingers glide down the man's face in an attempt to close the hollow dead eyes staring up at them.

Crystal put her hand on his arm gently. "You know that doesn't work in real life," she shook her head, "only in the movies partner, only in the movies." She stood and went to talk to the forensics team that had just gotten there.

Franco stared into the young man's eyes. The realization of what, he was sure was to come, steamrolled him. He got up and made his way outside to the balcony. Staring into the distance of the gray winter sky, he knew he had to pull himself together before Crystal saw how shaken he truly was. He knew what had come to their quite little piece of seaside paradise, what had drained all the blood from that poor bastard in there, but who? Who would be so careless, so stupid? It was one thing to break the laws of man but to go against the law of Vettorio was unheard of. It had been forbidden long ago to leave any trace of a vampire kill that might risk exposure.

She had to be one crazy bitch with a death wish. That thought conjured up only one name, "Selena." He nearly choked as he spat out her name. It had to be her.

137

He knew her all too well from his past life. She had always pushed her maker, the king, to his limits. Vettorio made many exceptions for his children, but Franco was certain this would not be something he would let pass. Once word got back to him and with two killings now, it would be soon if he did not know already, Vettorio would send his best hunter after Selena or worse, he would come himself.

Franco grasped hold of the railing looking up to the gray winter sky. He had no fear of Vettorio, but his life had been so much less complicated since he had found Maria and disappeared from everyone who knew him before. The idea of his own exposure was something he had always feared would come someday. He spoke with an anguished heart, choking back the lump forming in his throat. "Gods, please don't make me have to choose."

Crystal interrupted him. "What you doing out here?" She walked up next to him bumping her hip against his leg.

"I just needed some fresh air." He responded a little sharply.

"Well, all righty then." She snapped spinning around on her heels. Storming back inside and out the door she went.

"Crystal." Franco followed her. This was not the time for her short fuse. However, if there was the slightest chance he would be leaving here, leaving her, he did not want their last words to be harsh.

The camera flash bounced off Franco's eyes with a blinding haze that caught him off guard sending him spinning in the other direction for several seconds.

"Hey man, are you all right?" The photographer let his camera drop around his neck.

"Yeah man. You caught me good with that one." He forced a slight laugh. "Ask Braxton to put a rush on that and I'll be by his office to pick up the report later. No need to send it over. I want to put my hands on it ASAP."

"You've got it."

By the time Franco caught up to Crystal, she was sitting against the apartment wall near his car pouting. It's amazing how one can make pouting look like all hell was about to break loose. He could not help but smile at how sweet and innocent she looked pouting like his Isabella did when she was a toddler, yet another woman who could pout fiercely. This woman, the holy terror he loved beyond words. Words he had never dared speak to her, for reasons that failed him now, now that the future was so uncertain. He took a deep breath and walked around in front of her offering his hand to help her up.

She slapped it away. "Piss off DeLuca."

Franco backed away grinning, as he leaned back against the car. Folding his arms across his broad chest, he just stared at her making faces as he waited for her to get over herself. It took just a couple of minutes before she got up, brushed dirt from her butt and went to hug him. She still was not talking to him yet, she let him go quickly and got in the car, slamming the door. Franco got in and went for his box of cigars under the seat then decided against it. No need to piss her off worse by lighting up in the car.

"I will drop you at home. Take some aspirin or Midol and get some sleep. You look like shit." He prodded her in jest to cover the waves of emotion that were weighing heavy on him.

No response.

She was still pouting and that always meant the silent treatment. Franco turned to her making a face and sticking his tongue out at her. *"Essere un bambino allora.* Oh, excuse me Miss Harley. In English, be a baby then." He punched on his favorite 80's Monster Ballads CD then turned back to watch the road.

Crystal flipped her pinky finger at him.

"Oh, so I do not deserve the full bird today." He chuckled lightly. "You are never going to become a grown up." The words rolled off his tongue in his smooth slight Italian accent. He could not help but think about how much he loved her spirited little girl attitude about life, even as trying on his patience as she could be. He smiled at her as much with his eyes as he

141

did his perfect pearly whites. That always really pissed her off, more at herself than him.

She wanted him so badly it made her core tingle and ache as much as her heart did, every time she looked into those jade green eyes.

"November Rain" began to play. Crystal pulled her boots off and propped her feet up on the dash in front of her. She glanced at Franco out of the corner of her eye for a reaction. He equated the Nova to his lover. He had lavished her with attention and love until she purred with perfection and he lost his shit whenever he felt like Crystal was abusing his beloved classic, but she got no reaction.

"Really Franco, you know that song tears me up," she reached to change the song, but Franco caught her hand, pulling it away from the stereo.

Holding her hand under his, he rested their hands against the soft leather seat between them. The slight tremble she felt in his touch sent shivers up her spine causing her to pull back physically and emotionally.

She did not care if he noticed or even cared that she was pulling away. They could never have anything and she did not want to hand her heart to someone who would just hold it, looking at it, wondering what to do with it. Idle touches that were meant to be friendly were not allowed, as they were also confusing as hell. They both needed their heads in the game anyway. She was a strong woman who was not prone to girly fantasies and like she reminded him earlier, this was not a movie. Partners do not fall in love.

She turned away, staring out the window in silence. The rest of the drive to Crystal's house was very quiet. The silence she had created had become almost deafening to Crystal. Franco turned on to the long driveway, lined on either side with massive live oaks looming above that touched each other forming a Spanish moss covered canopy over the sandy driveway. She struggled to crank the window down in his black '69 Nova. "Oh yummy, the smell of the marsh at low tide, priceless." She waited a few seconds for a reaction that didn't come. "Damn it to hell Franco. I want you to

143

tell me what's up with you. You, the guy who would rather pick shit with the chickens, than do paperwork? Yeah, I heard you requesting this report in your hands, ASAP. You do not offer to take care of reports and I want to know why this one. What the holy fuck is going on inside that head of yours?"

The Nova stopped at her front steps. Franco leaned across her and opened the passenger door. "I'm just feeling overly generous today, princess. Enjoy it. Go get some sleep. You absolutely need it." Looking into her eyes while their faces were so close gave him a thrill, but he knew he could not lean forward and kiss her as he wanted to.

Crystal swallowed hard and then glared at him. "I'm so glad you became my mother. Get your face out of mine and back off. When you're ready to treat me as a partner, call me." Crystal got out with boots in hand, slammed the door, and leaned back into the window. "I don't know what your problem is Mister DeLuca but you can just piss off." She ran up the steps onto the wrap around porch of her two hundred year old family home that backed to the Atlantic. She stopped for a quick glance back at him over her shoulder flashing him a half smile that let him know she was not angry any longer, and then through the screen door into the house she went.

Franco watched her admiringly until she slammed the front door closed behind her. He drove off stopping at the end of her driveway to roll her window up and his down. Pulling an Ashton Magnum from the box under his seat, he slid the cigar under his nose breathing in the aroma of what he considered his one guilty pleasure. He lit the cigar, dug his cell phone out of the glove box and called his late wife, Maria's brother.

After the love of his life was killed in that car accident when Isabella was two, Franco needed to get away. He felt terrible taking his daughter away from her family, but the memories were too much for him to handle. He packed up his house he shared with his wife and daughter and moved to Beaufort.

It was no surprise to find Nick, Maria's brother on his doorstep a few weeks later. "An artist can paint anywhere." The tall slender young man told Franco when he showed up, standing there at the front door with all of his possessions in tow, a few items of clothing, artist paints and his beloved guitar. His daughter Isabella, though only two, could not have been happier that her uncle came to join them. Franco knew she missed her family in her own way and she did not understand what was going on. He could not begrudge her this, as he knew the feeling of missing loved ones, as well. It was not an imposition that Nick moved in with them. He enjoyed and loved Nick as much as he had once loved his own brother. In addition, to be honest, he could use the extra help with his daughter. He was afraid he might somehow screw up her life and he owed it to his beloved Maria to give her the best. Nevertheless, when she got older, Nick and Franco knew it was time for Nick to pick his life back up and he moved out on his own.

"Hello, my brother. I know it has been a while since I rang you. I am sorry for that. I need a bit of a favor." His speech was slow and deliberate.

"Anything you need, just name it." Their mutual love of Isabella had bonded the two men and Franco knew he could always count on Nick.

"I need you to come and take Isabella for a visit with her *la nonna e il nonno*. Can you do this for me, Nick?"

"Of course I will. You know I love spending time with my niece and I'm sure mom and dad would love to see her, but please tell me, is something wrong?" Nick felt an unfamiliar sense of foreboding in Franco's voice. Although he certainly had not kept Isabella from his family since Maria died, he had not offered her up to go back to New York just unexpectedly like this either. "How long are you thinking?"

Franco could feel the concern in Nick's tone. "There is no need for worry. I just have some stuff to work out and it would be better if you and she were to visit your *genitori* for a while. Can you do this for me without too many questions? I do not know the length of time to tell you. I will come there for her when it is finished."

"When should I plan on leaving?" Nick brushed loose strands of hair away from his face tucking it behind his ear with his long fingers.

"Tonight would be wonderful. I will have her ready," he checked his watch for the time, "say around half past seven? You can drive a few hours then spend the night, in Virginia maybe."

"Really? You're talking about tonight? Man you're scaring me."

"Please. Do not ask many questions. Just do this for me. You know I would not ask you if it were not important. I am trusting you, Nicky. You take *il mio bambino* and you watch over her like you never watched over anything in your life. Have you got me on this?"

Nick had an unshakable feeling Franco was leaving out much more than he was telling. Was Isabella in some kind of peril? He sucked in a breath and decided to respect his wishes without answers to the questions being fired off in his head. He had always trusted him like the older brother he had become. The slim twenty-eight year old would walk into a burning building if

Franco told him it was the thing to do. "Of course, I've got you covered. I'm packing now."

He made his way upstairs to the bedroom as they talked. The call ended. Nick tossed the phone on the bed. He pulled a suitcase from the closet and grabbed up some things. "What the holy fuck?" He questioned out loud pushing his fallen long streaked tresses away from clear blue eyes binding his hair in a ponytail. Calming himself down with a deep breath, he thought maybe this was just a case Franco was working on and he just would not have time to take care of Isabella. However, why was it so important she go to New York?

Franco arrived at the medical examiner's office, just as the now identified body of Travis Lee was being pushed inside the cold steel drawer. The Medical Examiner, Braxton, stopped in midstream and pulled the drawer back open when he saw Franco approaching.

"I've been expecting you," he pulled back the sheet covering the body and immediately started to run through the few facts he knew. "He was drained. That's the only Cause of Death I came up with. He bled out, emptied like somebody was about to do an embalming job on him." He paused shaking his head. "If I didn't know better, I would think there is something supernatural afoot here."

Franco raised a brow but let the comment go without response.

Braxton continued, "This mother was clean. And I do mean clean, not even an identifiable trace of DNA in the lipstick. It's like he was run through some kind of sterilizer or something just like the other guy. Crazy shit, this is." Braxton rolled Travis Lee over revealing long scratch marks down his shoulder blades. "These are fresh. They weren't post-mortem, what little bit of blood found at the scene came from these scratches." he let out a nervous laugh. "Hell of a way to go."

"Yeah really. So you don't have anything useful for me at this point?" Franco grabbed a pair of rubber gloves from the desk to give Travis Lee one final look over for himself. He examined the puncture wounds closely, breathing deeply in search of Selena's scent but got nothing.

"That would be a negative. The lab might find something on his clothes but I'd be surprised if they do and they still have not identified that lipstick brand" Braxton shrugged.

"What about those puncture wounds? Ever seen anything like that used before?" Franco shot Braxton a questioning glance.

"Nope. Just like the other one. Some type of syringe maybe, but we haven't matched it to anything yet." Braxton answered motioning to an array of syringes and ice picks spread out on a side table.

Pulling off the gloves Franco tossed them in the trash. "You'll call me if you come up with anything?" He knew they would not, but had to keep up appearances. He knew with every ounce of his being what *being* did this. Nevertheless, he would be ostracized if he started talking about vampires.

"Sure thing man." Braxton pulled the sheet back up over the body sliding the drawer shut with a thud that echoed throughout the sterile room. "Hey, where's the hottie with the potty mouth." He always flirted shamelessly with Crystal while she just ignored the tiny little ogre, as she described him.

Franco just shook his head and left. He sat in his car for several minutes smoking his cigar. He gathered his thoughts before driving to the office to file the report. He knew in his gut those puncture wounds were bite marks, no matter how badly he wanted it to be otherwise. But who would be so sloppy, so stupid. It had been forbidden for over a thousand years for any vampire to openly kill a human and risk exposure. To break Vettorio's law would mean certain death. He was asking himself the same questions over again. It had to be Selena. She was the only one he could think of that would be so defiant, so arrogant as to think she was above the king's laws.

He inhaled deeply letting the smoke drift up through his nose before blowing it back out along with a low deep growl. That crazy bitch had always been trouble and Franco never understood why Vettorio let her survive for so long. She had a part in every twisted disease or plague known to man in one way or another. The only thing that saved her from prosecution by the supreme council after the spread of the black plague was Vettorio. As Selena's maker, he had protected her for over three thousand years. If it were Selena then things would get very ugly, really fast.

As one of the original three daughters of Vettorio, Selena possessed unbelievable strength and cunning matched only by the hatred she had harbored for Franco since his altercation with her so many years ago.

He had to find a way to keep Crystal out of harm's way. If Selena saw her anywhere near him, it would make Crystal a prime target and he knew he no longer held the power to protect her, not against someone so powerful. Selena would take great pleasure in ripping out the throat of anyone close to Franco. She would know what Crystal meant to him. Nothing got past her, even emotions that were deeply hidden. He was even more certain now that sending Isabella and Nick away had been the right decision.

He pounded an open hand against the steering wheel. "I have to know for sure it is her before I do something I cannot undo." He growled into the air.

On the drive to the station, he would come up with whatever cock and bull story he could to get Sheriff Davis to mandate Crystal take some time off. It should not be too hard. Sheriff Davis trusted his judgment.

Monday morning Crystal breezed into the office all bright and happy doing, what Franco called, her Tigger bounce. Sheriff Davis motioned her to come in his office and shut the door.

"What's up, Cap?" She asked flopping down childlike in the big brown leather chair in front of his desk that dwarfed her in size.

"I want you to take some leave time. You have forfeited your vacation time for as long as I can remember and it's time you get away from here for a while." He walked around, leaned back against the desk and peered at her over his reading glasses. "Nope, don't want to hear it," he held his hand up to stop her before she spat the words out of her mouth. "Beginning today and for the next two weeks, I don't want to see you or so much as hear of you being anywhere near this office or any ongoing investigations. The holidays are just around the corner. Do some volunteer work; help your pop with Toys for Tots. I am sure he would welcome some time with you. Understood?"

"Understood? I need to know what grounds this is on. You know we are in the middle of an investigation and to pull me on this just because I have pushed off vacation is bullshit and you know it, sir."

"Listen. I have heard from the field that you have been losing your temper too often. I need everyone involved to have their head fully in the game and not be loose cannons. I need you to take my order as final and take some time off. There is something going on out there and I need to make sure everyone involved in the case, is up to par. I no longer think you are."

"Everyone loses their temper when they are not able to get the answers they need in order to take down the bad guy and keep them from killing others. This is bullshit and you know it!" She barked, storming out of the office barreling straight into Franco. "You fucking did this." She slammed both hands flat against his chest pushing him back a few feet.

"Settle down, princess. I don't know what's got you so worked up, but I assure you there is no conspiracy here." He took her hands off him and held on to them so she could not hit him again. "Just calm your little ass down and get a hold of yourself, so all these nice people here don't think you've gone off the deep end." He spoke softly trying to avoid the whole station hearing, but he was too late. All eyes were on them.

She took a deep breath and snatched her hands free of his. "All of y'all can just kiss my ass. I am outta here," and out the door she went. Crystal snatched her helmet off the seat of her purple Harley Davidson Street Glide and put it on tugging the strap tight under her chin. She was flinging obscenities for whoever wanted to hear. "Those fuckers piss me off so bad. I don't know why I even give a good shit." It did not go unnoticed by her that her partner did not come out after her. "Not a conspiracy, my ass." Straddling the motorcycle, and then stretching her legs out as far as they would go to reach the ground. She took off leaving a trail of smoke and the smell of burning rubber in the air.

6

The Meeting

BONAVENTURA HAD BEEN WATCHING FROM ACROSS THE STREET. He stood next to the dark tinted glass front of the coffee shop in his black leather jacket. Eyes squinted against the sun reflecting off the glass. He breathed in her scent as she sped past, not noticing him. He thought she smelled of roses, fresh linen and sunshine in spring, this strange creature with her brash attitude and vulgar mouth. He was intrigued, to say the least, though he had not a clue why.

In his long existence, there had been thousands of women to come and go yet he had never given a second thought to any of them. What was so intoxicating about this human he had not even come to know? What he did know was she may be able to help him with the Selena problem.

Selena was covering her trail. That horrid perfume that carried the stench of skunk urine she had sprayed to throw anyone searching for her off her trail, was working. She was the most dangerously cunning of his siblings with a grotesque taste for cat and mouse games. Vettorio had sent him to track her because he was the only one, other than the king himself, capable not only of finding her, but subduing her once he had. His orders were to bring her back to Bozen to be taken to the Aesir to face the council, once and for all. If necessary, he was to end her on the spot.

It would have troubled Bonaventura to even consider such a task were it either of his other sisters, but not Selena. She hated him from the day he was born and had been nothing but cruel to him. Vettorio banished her from Italy when he was a child not allowing her to come back until he was grown and could defend himself. She had kept her distance from him after being allowed to return home with Vettorio promising to kill her if she ever laid hands on him again. Her hatred and jealousy of him continued to grow and fester over the centuries.

Vettorio had heard about the killings going on here and around the world. Americans seemed to be fascinated with vampires and the king knew it was time to step in before the rumors started swirling and a craze started among the humans. This is how Bonaventura found himself in the town of Beaufort, in the state of South Carolina. It was very difficult to track her here and he wasn't certain she was still here, or if this was the work of her minions. But one look at that sexy cop and overhearing her rant, he knew she was the one to approach.

He needed to know what the cops knew and he figured Crystal was as good a place as any to start. In a flash, he had followed her scent out to her house on the southeastern shore. He watched from a grove of oaks as she stomped and kicked her way across the porch and into the house. Her show of fiery temper made him smile. He thought he liked this outlandish creature and might enjoy seducing her. What harm was there in a little sport as long as he accomplished the task at hand. He leaned against a massive live oak and waited.

It was only a few minutes before Crystal reappeared on the front porch. Tugging her ponytail through the hole in the back of an orange baseball cap with Tigers printed across the front. She sat down on the wooden steps of the spacious old white board house with its railings draped in evergreens and white lights for the holidays. Angrily shoving her feet into a pair of purple rain boots, she was still barking under her breath. She pulled the boots over the legs of her worn black jeans. The orange and white striped sweater she had on over her purple turtleneck was so big on her that the neckline was falling off her shoulders. Bonaventura wondered if it belonged to a boyfriend or a husband.

"Here Charlie, come on boy let's go," she called out clapping her hands and the black Lab came running to her, tail wagging and licking her in the face. "You silly baby. I love you. Yes, I do."

Bonaventura saw her smile for the first time. She spoke to the dog in baby talk making kissing motions in the air and rubbing his head. Charlie stopped, his head held high, he sniffed the air and growled showing his teeth.

"What's wrong buddy?" Crystal looked around but saw nothing. "Come on you big baby, let's go play." She started toward the beach behind the house. Charlie followed with the hairs standing up on his back.

Crystal had been running and playing fetch with Charlie for a couple of hours before Bonaventura decided the timing was right to approach her. That canine could be trouble for him so he proceeded with caution, keeping a sense of the dog's emotions as he walked closer.

Charlie spotted him first. Running out of Crystal's sight he charged snarling full force at him. Bonaventura caught him, hands braced against the dog's shoulders. He held him away with just enough pressure, to keep the dog from doing any damage with those sharp teeth Charlie fully intended to sink into his throat.

He smiled respectfully. "It's all right my friend. I know you are just protecting her. I mean her no harm." He whispered calmly. "For fuck's sake, by the blood of the gods I can't believe I am doing this." Another time and he might have broken the dog's neck and been done with it. However, that would get him nowhere with his owner and he needed her right now. He needed her knowledge of the murders that were happening. He went to his knees holding Charlie around his neck with one hand and under his chin with the other. Gazing eye to eye with the dog until the glamour was completed. By the time Crystal caught up, Charlie and Bonaventura were playing tug of war together with a piece of driftwood.

"Hi there. I see you've met Charlie. I'm Crystal." She offered her hand. He caught her tiny hand and placed a lingering kiss on her knuckles.

"Bonaventura, it is my pleasure to make your acquaintance, *Fräulein*." He took her in admiringly from head to toe. She was even more petite close up than he had thought her to be from a distance, and quite beautiful in a quirky sort of way.

"I'm sorry, Bonna what?" She squished up her whole face, a puzzled look taking over.

"Bo-nah-ven-too-rah. It's Latin. It means good fortune or some shit like that. My parents are very old fashioned that way. If you know what I mean? So I got stuck with an archaic name." He laughed flashing what she thought was the most flawless of smiles.

The words rolled off his tongue with a smooth silky accent similar to Franco's that she found very sexy. She recognized the German from all the old episodes of Rat Patrol she had suffered through with her dad. "You have a beautiful accent. Where are you from? How about if I just call you Vent? Would that be okay?" She fired off her questions without giving him a chance to answer then took a breath. She returned his smile. "Your turn."

"Certainly, you may call me Vent if it pleases you." He caught her gaze and held it as he continued small talk in an attempt to win her over. "My family comes from a small village in Northern Italy called Bozen." Noting her puzzled look returning, he explained further. "Bozen is near the German border just below the alps. Most of the people there speak German although some Italian or such as myself, both languages are native. It is a very beautiful little village." His smile spread. "That is quite an accent you have there yourself, *Fräulein.*"

"I'm just a little bit Southern," she giggled. "Would you care to join us for a walk?"

"It would be my pleasure." He held his arm up in a bent position and she quickly snaked hers around it, and they walked forward with Charlie close on their heels.

The nip in the air was growing sharper, colder than normal for December in Beaufort. The breeze coming off the Atlantic that traveled across the marsh carried a thick salty smell and taste that assaulted Bonaventura's keen senses. He quickened their pace until they were back out onto the open beach.

"So what is it you do to make your living, Miss Crystal?" he quirked a brow releasing her arm and spinning on his heels to face her as he continued to walk slowly backwards, "It is Miss, is it not?"

"Oh yes, it is Miss for sure. But please call me Crystal or CJ" She smiled tilting her head back slightly to make eye contact with him from beneath the brim of her cap. "I am a detective with the Beaufort County Sheriff's Department." She watched for the usually shocked response.

He feigned a slight look of surprise. "CJ? You do not look much like I would expect for a person of law enforcement."

"Crystal Jane Harley is my full name but I don't brag on it." She laughed.

"I rather like Crystal, it suits you. Your eyes sparkle like Austrian crystals and emeralds when the sun hits

166

just right up under there." He stopped and pulled her cap back slightly.

"Stop that." She giggled pushing his hand away and readjusting her cap. "There's no sparkle in these jaded eyes, I assure you."

"Nonsense, I see it as does everyone else, I am sure."

Crystal was starting to wonder whom this man was that came out of nowhere. She knew better than to run her mouth and give out details about her life freely. She had seen too many women who met strangers and made that mistake. She knew she could take care of herself, but there was also something about this man that made her wonder exactly how dangerous he could be. He was charming to be sure and knew all the right words to say to a woman. Maybe she should watch herself a bit more, but she found it was easy to talk to him, this stranger.

Charlie ran ahead chasing after a fiddler crab then racing back he jumped up on Bonaventura from behind, catching him off guard, knocking him off balance. He stumbled and both he and Crystal fell to the sand beneath them in a heap, with Charlie barking as if laughing at them.

"Charlie! Bad boy, shame on you." Crystal laughed. Charlie nudged his head back between them licking her in the face.

Bonaventura rolled off of her on to his back looking up at the cloudy gray sky. "It looks like a storm may be brewing. Perhaps we would be well advised to start back."

Crystal sat upright with Charlie resting his head in her lap. She looked up to the sky with a big grin while rubbing Charlie's ears. "I am so really lovin' the way you talk. All smooth and proper like, you could give a Southern country girl a complex or somethin'. Yep it's fixin' to storm. I can smell it in the air and from the looks of those clouds there," pointing out toward the water at a group of dark gray and pink storm clouds, "I would say there may well be some ice involved." She laughed getting up, dusting the sand from her bottom. Cupping her butt cheeks in her hands she said, "Damn, my ass is frozen now." Turning her back to him,

"Would you mind terribly? I'll dust yours if you'll dust mine," she smirked.

Bonaventura was finding himself oddly mystified by this strange female. In his long life and travels, he had never come across anyone quite like her. She was indeed like a shot of the strongest Irish whiskey poured into the finest crystal champagne flute. Uniquely beautiful but filled with an unexpected kick. He felt the edges of his lips tugging into a grin and the fit of his jeans tightening from the bulge of his manhood pressing to escape the confines of his pants as he brushed the sand off the back of her sweater. To his surprise, he found he had to concentrate profusely to calm his arousal before she turned around and found his attraction to her visibly obvious.

He had learned nothing about the murders and for just a moment considered getting what he needed from her mind but he didn't want to simply glamour her or invade her mind and walk away. It was he that was being compelled. He had an almost irresistible pull to her. To just be near her was preventing him from his usual trickery. He was struggling to comprehend exactly what was going on. There were strange emotions at work, something he had never experienced before.

Once the bulk of the damp sand had been brushed away they headed back toward Crystal's, they had been walking and making small talk for hours. The sun had disappeared into the sea below the horizon, and the creamy foam of the breakers glistened beneath a clear, nearly full moon as the high tide claimed the sandy shore by the time they made their way back to her property.

A light sleet began to dance off the walk as they approached the house, prompting them to take the steps three at a time in a leap to the shelter of the covered porch, laughing. Charlie jumped into a nearby rocking chair. Resting on his paws he tilted his eyes up at them with a strange sort of amused look watching them taking each other in.

They had just met, yet she felt as if she had jumped into one of her childhood fairytale books and he was her Prince Charming, with his dark sultry eyes that she could have sworn twinkled in the moonlight. He was taller than she, but not really tall. She thought him quite muscular with prominent cheekbones, a cute ski sloped nose that was not unlike her own, but much more adorable. The most inviting sexy pink lips she had ever seen spoke in an intoxicating rhythm that rolled off his lips in waves, leaving her near drunk. Lips she was already longing to feel pressed hard against her own. She suspected he was at least five years her junior maybe even ten years but for once she was strangely all right with that, and didn't even care to question his age.

"Well then, I bid you good night." He brought her hand to his lips peering over her knuckles into her clear green eyes. In that moment the realization, that Crystal's eyes were the exact color of his mother's, brought sudden warmth to his heart. His words were saying good night but he did not want to leave. He had the strangest sense of belonging there, with this brash fiery red head.

A part of her wanted to ask him to come inside but the cop in her thought it was a bad move, so she said her good night at the door. She let Charlie in the house then turned back to Bonaventura. "If you don't have any plans, you could come to dinner tomorrow. Say around seven?"

Bonaventura felt a smile bloom on his lips. "Seven sounds good." He watched her until the door shut behind her.

Crystal tossed and turned in a restless sleep, lost in the most surreal dream she'd ever experienced. She was near the top of a mountain. It was covered in snow but she did not feel cold. Looking down at herself her white silk and lace dress was blowing lightly around her legs; the sheer sleeves were incrusted with tiny crystals and pearls. Could it be a bridal gown? A noise caught her attention and she looked up. In the distance, she could just make out a castle. Bonaventura suddenly appeared out of nowhere. He was staring at her with his lips pressed together in a half smile. The black leather pants he wore

172

were just tight enough to show off his muscular thighs. His crisp white shirt was tucked in but unbuttoned, Platinum and diamond cuff links held his sleeves snugly at his wrists. She reached her hand out to him but quickly snatched it back. Her heart was in a tug of war with her head. He came closer taking her hand, kissing it tenderly and dropping to one knee. When he gazed up over her knuckles, his eyes were blazing red. Crystal let out a gasp in fear. She wanted to run but she could not move.

"Wake up damn it," she told herself.

His eyes returned to their normal dark pools looking at her with a longing that burned through her soul. She felt herself involuntarily sink to her knees, arms around his neck. Just as their lips parted against each other... her alarm went off.

Crystal's eyes popped open wide. She was covered in sweat, clenching the sheet in her hands "What the holy fuck?" She screamed knocking the alarm to the floor. His image was still burning brightly in her mind. His intoxicating eyes were inviting her into his very existence. He was real she knew he was, they had met only yesterday. Why did he have such an affect on her, this mystery man? What was the significance of those red eyes, and why did she feel such a strong pull toward him? A multitude of questions popping off in her head like the rapid fire of an M-16 sent her diving in a scream under the pillows.

Bonaventura had been searching the coast from Beaufort to Charleston and back all night for any trace of his sister. He was very restless and pissed off when he got back to his hotel room. Falling on the bed, he closed his eyes for a minute and *found himself emerging from behind a large boulder. He was in his favorite place in the world, high in the Alps beyond his father's castle. Crystal was there just above him in a small clearing. She looked beautiful, almost magical.*

He jumped up from the bed and went to wash his face.

What the hell is going on? He could sense that it was a dream, her dream but who was drawing him into it and why? When he looked up from the sink *he was once again clearly there on the mountain* in the mirror.

He slammed an open hand against the wide expanse of mirror shattering it. "I will not be manipulated by anyone!" He growled backing up sliding down the wall to the tiled floor. Drawing his knees up to his chest he bowed his head into his crossed arms on top of his knees.

As soon as he closed his eyes he was back in Crystal's dream and *kneeling in front of her.* He was fighting it in his mind but the pull was too strong even for him with his exceptionally gifted mindset. He decided to go with it and cautiously see where it led. *He could taste her skin when his lips touched her hand. He felt a huge void ripped in time when their lips came so close he could inhale her breath just as she disappeared from his mind.*

He got up hoping a shower would clear his head. Standing under the hot water, letting it run over his face he struggled to make sense of what had just happened. He was the only vampire he knew of that had the gift of invading someone's mind and controlling their thoughts like that. What he experienced was not like being glamoured, not at all.

Why had he felt so drawn to her last night? She was nothing special, as far as he could see; yet he found himself completely in awe of her emerald eyes, fiery tresses and spitfire attitude. It had taken all his will to walk away from her. He had to find out what the hell was happening and to do so he needed to see her again. He grinned at the thought; of course, he would see her again. He had decided that before he ever left her house. He would travel into her mind if need be when he accepted her dinner invitation.

He got dressed and went to see the concierge to arrange to rent a car for the sake of appearances. David Cooper, the hotel concierge, made the call for him and arranged for a Town car to drive him to the rental lot.

Bonaventura drove to the Sheriff's office. The building was buzzing with chatter making it easy for him to flash past the deputies in the outer office unnoticed. He quickly scanned the reports on the murders then took off with no trace of ever being there.

He parked a couple of blocks from the apartment of Travis Lee. Being careful not to be seen, he made his way into the stairwell and up to the apartment. Once he opened the door he could feel Selena's lingering energy, it was faint but definitely her. The horrid shit she had sprayed in the room assaulted his keen sense of smell to the point he felt physically ill.

"Holy mother of fuck!" He called out between coughs.

Searching the apartment quickly with no results Bonaventura attempted to pick up her scent to track her from the apartment. He stomped around brooding for several minutes once he got back outside in the fresh air.

He was at a loss, the best tracker known to the vampire kingdom and I do not have a fucking clue what direction my crazy bitch sister took from here.

Their dinner plans were for seven but Bonaventura found he could not wait, patience had never been a virtue of his and he arrived at five. It was dusk, Crystal and Charlie were returning from a walk on the beach.

"Well hello there." She flashed him a half smile.

"I know I am a bit early but I thought perhaps I could help you prepare our meal." He grinned wide.

Crystal opened the door. Charlie ran in. She and Vent followed. He built a fire in the fireplace while she made a pot of coffee. Bonaventura watched as Charlie pulled his bright blue fuzzy blanket from the chair and walked in circles in front of a huge Christmas tree to the side of the fireplace until he was wrapped in his blanket with only his eyes peering out.

"He is pretty smart, your dog." Vent took the cup of coffee she held out to him walking back into the living room.

"Sometimes he is just too damned smart, if you know what I mean?" She motioned for him to sit with her on the overstuffed beige cotton sofa that faced the fire. Charlie was peeking up at them from the edge of his blanket. They had their coffee before gathering around the kitchen island. He put together a salad while she boiled the pasta to go with the sauce she already had simmering in a crock-pot.

They sat at the island and exchanged small talk while they ate. Bonaventura pondered the best way to approach her about the dream while he ate his spaghetti. He did not wish to frighten her but he needed answers.

They enjoyed a leisurely meal and afterward he offered to help with the dishes. She did not hesitate to accept. He was surprised he actually found himself enjoying the banter and childish play that ensued during the clean up. He had never cleaned a dish in his long life and was quite amused with himself over it. When she invited him to stay and watch a movie, he didn't hesitate.

They shared a half-gallon of Moose tracks ice cream, which they ate out of the carton along with a bowl of popcorn Crystal insisted had to be eaten together while watching, "When Harry Met Sally." They watched movies, played tug a war with the sofa pillows, talked and giggled like little kids most of the night.

It had not been necessary to glamour her. Quite the contrary, he felt as though it were he who was under her spell. Vent watched her sleep in his arms on the sofa and almost forgot his reason for being there, or at least the reason he had told himself he was going to get to know her. He brushed her hair away from her face with his fingers and kissed her forehead holding his lips pressed against her soft skin, breathing her in.

"What crazy thing is this that you are doing *blödmann*," he whispered to himself finding it impossible to move from the sofa, to slip away like he knew was the smart thing to do. He did not even care that sex had not come into play. Not yet. Wow, what a first. He, the guy that fucked his way around the world more than a few times was content with just a snuggle. He smirked at himself. In his position, as Vettorio's son and heir, pretty much every female vampire in the world had offered to be his mate. With his sultry good looks, there had been as many humans in his bed, as well. Sex was simply an amusing way to pass the time to him, until he looked into Crystal's eyes and for the first time he felt something more than just a hard-on. He pondered his feelings while watching her sleeping so peacefully. The dream had retuned to her. He could see what she was seeing in his mind. But this time he felt at ease with it. She shifted and snuggled deeper into his embrace before waking up.

"Good morning." Crystal glanced up. The sun shined through the window like a big spotlight against his handsome face and those beautiful almost black eyes she so easily could get lost in. "I had the most surreal dream." She hesitated not sure if she should share it with him. She looked down.

He sensed her concern. "You might think I am crazy, I won't blame you if you do but I had a strange dream as well. We were together in the mountains of my homeland." He lifted her chin with his index finger until she met his gaze. In her eyes he saw a fear and longing that touched him in a way he had never experienced, and that frightened him just a little.

Cupping her cheeks in his hands he spoke in a low tone, "I honestly do not understand what connection there is between us Crystal Jane Harley, but I think it a folly to ignore."

For several seconds all she could manage was a small nod in agreement. She had never been in love, nothing more than the usual teenage crush. Even as strong as her feelings for Franco had become she wasn't sure it was love, not the real forever kind little girls dream about. Why was she being overtaken by emotions by this stranger? It excited her and scared the hell out of her at the same time. She suddenly needed some space or she was going to suffocate.

"I'm going to put some coffee on." She slipped out of his arms, dashed off to the kitchen, put the coffee on and ran to the bathroom to brush her teeth. When she got back to the living room, he was gone. Her heart sank until she heard the water running in the guest bath. Crystal went to find him in the shower. "Mind if I join you?" She purred pulling the curtain back admiring washboard perfect abs.

"It is your house. Come on in." He smirked. She stepped in the shower and straight into his embrace. He covered her face and neck with little butterfly kisses. When his mouth finally connected with hers, the depth of passion fired up in both of them was almost unbearable. He picked her up in his arms pushing her back against the shower wall, as she locked her legs tightly around his waist. The hot water was pounding against their flesh. He eased inside of her soft folds. At first slowly then he picked up the pace to match the rocking of her hips against him. Crystal intertwined both hands in his hair pulling his mouth even closer, until their tongues danced deeply in her throat.

She moved her hips even harder matching his pace, riding him until she cried out in pleasure. "Oh my God, Vent." She moaned. He turned the faucet off and let her slide down off him before picking her up and carrying her to the bed. Tossing her down on the bed with a giggle, he began kissing her toes, working his way up her legs until he was between her thighs. Crystal arched her back, clenching the pillow with both hands. Vent's experienced tongue and fingers were taking her places she had never been, never even imagined before. He rolled over pulling her along and nudging her to an upright position where she took the lead, holding on by his nipples until they had both reached astonishing climaxes. Crystal collapsed against his chest. "Wow. Just wow." She panted.

"Me, too." Vent responded wrapping his arms around her, kissing her forehead. They lay there totally spent just holding each other for almost an hour.

"I have to pee and I am starving," Crystal broke the silence. She gave him a quick peck on the lips and ran off to the bathroom taking the half-soaked top sheet along, wrapped around her.

Charlie came running into the bedroom barking to be fed. Vent followed him to the kitchen. He found a bag of dog food, "That was pretty fucking amazing my friend." his whole face lit up with his smile. "Pretty fucking amazing indeed," he poured the food in Charlie's bowl and rubbed him on the head.

Crystal walked into the kitchen in her robe. Charlie was chowing down and Vent was at the stove putting bacon in a frying pan. "You may want these." She dangled his red boxer briefs in front of him. "We wouldn't want a little grease splatter to ruin your day." She gave him a quick peck on the cheek and a slap on his naked ass.

He raised an eyebrow at her and slipped into his underwear.

Taking a bowl from the cabinet and grabbing eggs from the fridge she asked, "May I help?" They finished cooking and had breakfast picnic style on the fake bear rug covering the heart pine living room floor in front of the fireplace.

Vent could not take his eyes off her. She possessed a captivating beauty he had never noticed in a woman before, and definitely never expected to find when he followed Selena here. For the first time, he truly understood what his father had told him about no longer having free will once his mother came into his life.

When he was young, Vettorio took him into the Alps to hunt and he would tell him stories of how he had found Althea on those church steps, what it meant to know the true love of a soul mate, and if he were patient, Bonaventura, too, would someday feel that depth of passion for his own mate. His true mate. The one woman the gods fated him to have. His father made it all sound so pleasant, in a life in which Bonaventura had only felt alone in his darkness. After nearly twelve hundred years he had all but given up on ever knowing what it felt like. That strange and wonderful emotion he had heard so much about. He had always admired what his parents had found in one another. After all these centuries together, they still looked at each other longingly, lustfully and with an insurmountable amount of mutual respect.

"What are you studying about so hard?" Crystal interrupted his thoughts.

"Pardon me?" He touched his hand to her knee not following her question.

"What are you thinking about silly?" She took his hand in hers.

"Just how absolutely perfect you look sitting here in front of the fire."

He got up on his knees moving their cups and plates to the coffee table. Vent leaned in untying her robe with his teeth. She snaked her arms around his neck, as she lay back on the rug pulling him to her eager mouth. He met her kiss then pulled back looking deeply into those green eyes. "You smell like sunshine," he whispered before capturing her mouth again with his. Vent rolled over and in one smooth motion, he was in a sitting position with Crystal's legs wrapped around his waist moving her hips to the rhythm of her quickening heartbeat. Before she knew it, he had picked her up. And her back was against the living room wall. The sudden sound of blowing sleet crashed against the metal roof and startled them both into a laugh.

Their lovemaking came to a climactic pause in room after room until Crystal found herself exhausted and sitting on the edge of the kitchen island. She was

187

struggling to catch her breath. Vent feigned heavy breathing. "I'm starving. How about you?" Crystal asked between breaths.

"I think you are always starving." Vent grabbed an egg turner from the utensil bucket on the island and slid it under her hip laughing.

"Oh Jesus, my naked ass is on this bar. I have to eat here." She pushed him away sliding off the marble island top laughing hysterically.

Vent's cell phone interrupted in a loud blaze of classical music that warned him it was Vettorio calling.

"Seriously?" she made a face at the music.

"I'm sorry. I must take this call." He walked to the living room to get his pants on while he answered the call.

"Have you found her?" Vettorio's voice was strong and to the point "Has it been handled?"

"No sir." Vent answered respectfully. "Not yet, but..."

"Do I need to intervene?" Vettorio cut him off.

Vent looked to be sure Crystal was still in the kitchen and could not hear. "Selena has been crafty in her cover up. But I assure you I can and will handle her. I will call you when it is finished, and when I am on my way back to Bozen. *Vertrauen Sie mir, mit diesem Vater. Ich werde Euch nicht enttäusche.* (Trust me with this father. I will not disappoint you.)"

"As your father, of course I trust you and I know you would never fail me as your king." Vettorio concluded the call leaving Bonaventura feeling like his father was there in the room with him.

He finished dressing, explained to Crystal he had business in town but would return by dark if that were all right with her.

"Sure. I'll cook something nice." She grinned.

"As nice as breakfast I hope." With a long deep kiss, he said goodbye.

7

Bitter Sweet Reunion

FRANCO WAS WALKING TO THE PIER SIPPING AN EXTRA-LARGE BLACK COFFEE, PUFFING ON HIS CIGAR, HEADED TOWARD YET ANOTHER CRIME SCENE. He slipped on his shades to shield his eyes from the blazing midday sun that felt hot against his face even in this winter cold spell. He stopped at the edge of the pier to question the harbormaster "Morning Mack. How is the family? What can you tell me?"

"Fine, thanks. Those guys were fishing this morning." The portly sixty-year-old man motioned to three men leaning against the railing at the far end of the pier. "Said they didn't see him there at first. It was still pretty dark when they first came out. Anyway, he was just sort of sitting on the decking leaned against that bench over there." He pointed to the body slumped over in a dark gray pea coat and matching stocking cap.

The coroner's office was already on the scene taking pictures. Braxton was standing next to the body. Franco made his way to the crime scene area. "Talk to me Braxy." Franco tamped out the cigar against the sole of his boot.

"Really DeLuca?" He snapped. "Ya gonna contaminate my crime scene." Braxton shooed him back.

"You are so full of the shit. Just tell me. Are we looking at a serial or no?"

"Yes, but this one apparently got screwed without getting screwed, if you catch my drift. He has the same puncture wounds, the red lipstick, and that same gross

191

ass odor is on him." Braxton waved his hand in front of his nose.

Franco watched the forensics crew finish up. He squatted down on his ankles to do his own exam of the body. The strong smell seared his nose hairs and made him feel physically ill, prompting him to stand back up and take a deep breath. A sudden breeze from the west slapped him dead in the face with her scent. He gave the parking lot a quick look over, but no sign of her. That scent was Selena. He was sure of it, even beneath that ghastly perfume. She had to be near. Had she seen him? Smelled him as he had her? He certainly hoped not. He wasn't ready to face a vampire of her age with the abilities she possessed. Worst-case scenario, her hatred of him would mean his human death as soon as she saw him. At best, Vettorio would learn he still lives, and he had been living as a human being these past years in secret while King Vettorio had thought him destroyed. For Christ's sake, this was going to get fucking ugly.

Franco motioned for Braxton's crew to take the body away. Franco walked around the parking lot several times looking for any other traces of Selena. The original three female vampires made by Vettorio have the ability to walk in the day without fear, although they usually avoid bright sun just because it was so harsh on their eyes, even through dark sunglasses. He did not find anything. Her scent had faded. Although his senses were not what they used to be, he was picking up something else in the air. It was a familiar scent he could not place, but it made the hairs on the back of his neck stand up and gave him an uneasy feeling deep in his gut.

Once he was confident she was nowhere around, he went to the Nova, sat down behind the wheel, re-lit his cigar and called to make sure Nick and Isabella had gotten to New York safely, and all was well. As he was listening to the phone ringing, he thought it was a blessing that CJ was off duty as well. He didn't want another person to worry about. CJ would go into this headstrong and blind. He did not need that on his plate as well.

Isabella raced to get the phone before Nick. "Hello. This is Bella."

"Hello, il mio bambino dolce."

"Daddy, I am not a baby anymore, don't you know?"

"Yes. I am sorry, my sweet young lady. Better?" The sound of her voice warmed his heart and a half smile blossomed across his lips.

"Thank you, kind sir." She snickered. "Are you coming to grandmas now? I miss you bunches already. We are going to see the Christmas lights and maybe ice skating tomorrow night." Her big bright eyes sparkled at the thought of Franco joining them.

Tears began to well up in his eyes fearing that he may never see his baby girl again. "Not just yet sweetheart. Daddy loves you, *zucca*. I hope it is still okay to call you my pumpkin?" He rubbed the inside corners of his eyes. Catching the bridge of his nose between his thumb and index fingers he bowed his head.

"Of course, that was mommy's name. I like it when you call me *zucca*." She flashed a big smile he could feel in her voice. "I love my Papa. I have the bestest papa in the whole world." She beamed in her best Shirley Temple impersonation. Every Saturday morning since Isabella was three they had piled up in Franco's bed in their PJs with a big bowl of popcorn and a box of tissues to watch old Shirley Temple movies together. "Uncle Nick promised he would do the tap dance with me. We are watching The Little Colonel Saturday. He tries really hard Papa, but he can't do it the same as you do." She laughed a big belly giggle. "I love you to the moon and around the whole universe." She made circling motions with her free hand up in the air.

He wiped away the tears that had escaped despite his struggle to hold them back. Forcing a slight laugh, "I have a superstar *figlia*. I love you so very, very much my *zucca*." He ended their call with kisses into the phone.

Franco got a call that a suspect had been picked up for questioning. He knew it could not possibly be the murderer that he sought, but he needed to go through the motions of a normal investigation, so he drove to the office.

He was sitting at the table in the interview room when Franco got there. David Bonds looked to be about sixty with greasy gray hair and a beard. He leaned over the table tapping his thumbs against the tabletop and rocking his upper torso back and forth.

Sheriff Davis walked up just before Franco entered the room. "Looks like he might shit his pants if you yelled boo when you walk in there."

"You don't really figure him for this do you?"

"Hell no. But the old bastard knows something. I'd bet on that." Sheriff Davis walked on as Franco went inside.

"Mr. Bonds you were seen running away from the pier at four this morning. What were you doing down there?" He began the questions before reaching the table.

Bonds looked up "I...I was meeting a friend." He stammered. He began nervously twirling his thumbs around one another with his fingers locked tightly together.

"And does said friend have a name?"

Mr. Bonds was visibly terrified. "It don't matter none." He began ringing his hands together. "Can I go now? I don't know nothin', mister. I swear to God I don't know nothin' and I didn't see nothin' either."

"I don't recall asking if you saw anything, Mister Bonds. But since you brought it up, why don't you tell me what you *didn't* see." Franco walked around behind Bonds. He put an open hand on the older man's shoulder leaning in really close. "You did see her," he whispered.

David Bonds went pale, eyes widened. "No, you're wrong. I told you I didn't see nothin'."

It was clear to Franco this man did indeed see something or someone, and it scared the living hell out of him. He would not push Bonds too hard right now because he did not want anyone else to know what the man may have seen of Selena. Franco felt the fewer people who knew about her, the better. The poor son-of-a-bitch had no idea how lucky he was to be sitting here right now. Selena had not seen him or else he wouldn't be. She must be getting sloppy, which is even a worse scenario than he first imagined. Franco would see that Bonds was cut loose and then corner him for the whole story away from the station, away from any ears he did not want to share this knowledge.

Franco assured the Sheriff, Mister Bonds was useless and they should cut him loose. After some routine paperwork, that is what they did. David Bonds had walked three blocks when Franco came up beside him steering him into Faye's Diner. Ordering two coffees, he guided Bonds to take a seat in the booth at the back of the room. The tiny little diner had emptied out the lunch crowd, so there were only a few people still seated inside, a couple of salesmen and a group of teens he surmised were out of school for winter break. They took seats on either side of a worn red leather booth. Franco crossed his arms and just looked at Bonds for several seconds before speaking. "I know you saw her this morning." He nodded his head.

"I don't know who you think I saw, but you're wrong. I want to speak to a lawyer."

"There's no need for that. You and I," he waggled his finger back and forth between them, "we are just sitting here having a friendly conversation man to man." He leaned over the edge of the table pulling a cigar from his jacket pocket offering it to Bonds.

Bonds took the cigar, breathed in the aroma and tucked it away in his pocket. "Look here, Captain, I don't want any trouble with you guys." He started to get up.

Franco caught him by the arm pulling him back into the booth. "It's Lieutenant and you have no idea the shitstorm you're in mister." He leaned in close speaking in a whisper, "If she caught the slightest glimpse of you or smelled you, which was likely, given you are a bit gamey. Well, mister you do not wanna know the things she will do to you. Let me help you. I can hide you out for a while." Franco took him by his hands over the tabletop and looked him straight in the eyes squeezing the man's hands between his own.

"You don't have to try to frighten me. Them red devil eyes of hers done that well enough. No sir, I got the fear of God put in me but good." Looking around to be sure no one was listening. "What ya wanna know? You give me your word not to tell I told ya. People will think me crazy; maybe even have me put away."

Franco nodded in agreement. "Just describe what you saw, what she looked like from the beginning."

"Me and my old buddy, Thomas was meetin' at the pier, gonna go see about a job later on that new boat we seen docking yesterday. He had gotten there before me and was walking out on the pier. We liked to watch the ships going in and out from the docks across the sound. Any ways, when I come up I seen her with him. I thought Thomas might be making time with her, ya know? Took a peek with my binoculars. I'd brought

200

them along for looking at the ships in the sound. Blood all over that pale, white face and them red eyes. Never gonna forget them eyes long as I live, no sir." He pulled loose from Franco's grip. Washing his face with his hands, he tried to clear the lump from his throat. "What in God's name was that she-devil mister?"

"That pretty much sums her up. Now finish telling me what she looked like, what color was her hair? Was she tall, thin, short, fat?"

"She was average height, I guess. She had sandy blonde hair down round her shoulders. Had on the reddest lipstick. And fangs, she had mother-fucking fangs. Like in the movies she did. Till she went all bat shit crazy on Tom, I thought she were a pretty girl. Much too pretty and too young to be talking to the likes of Tom. Twenty-five maybe thirty she was and him near fifty. Was near fifty, God rest his soul." Bonds bowed his head and crossed himself. "Nobody would ever believe. They'll be thinkin' I'm crazy."

Franco explained to Bonds that he had a cabin in the mountains just outside of Maggie Valley, North

Carolina. He would put him up there for safekeeping. He hoped it would not become necessary to use him as bait. That little bit of information he would keep to himself.

Bonaventura turned the corner just as Franco was ushering Bonds into the Nova. He stopped dead in his tracks, his eyes widened in disbelief. "Holy fucking shit!" He ducked back around the edge of the corner drug store. Wiping his eyes with his coat sleeve, he whispered to himself, "Holy...Fucking...Shit." He shook his head hanging on each word. Slowly he peeked back around the corner. Franco was getting in the driver's side of his Nova. Bonaventura flashed to the rental he had picked up to avoid too many questions from Crystal. Easing the red Ford in behind the Nova, he followed them at a distance to Franco's house. "I did not see this one coming. Holy fucking shit." He kept repeating those three words repeatedly aloud to himself, shaking his head in disbelief. He parked about a mile from the house then quietly flashed to outside the house on foot. An endless string of questions bounced around inside his head. Could Michael feel his presence? He took a deep breath. Why hadn't he picked up even a hint of his scent in the air or felt his presence? Bonaventura had always felt him anytime they were within miles of each other. How had Michael masked himself so well and why? They had thought him destroyed, had grieved for his loss. It had been the only time in all of his long life that Bonaventura had seen his father cry or lose control of his temper. Bloody tears stained the king's face for months.

Countless vampires were tortured and killed because they were suspected to have been hiding knowledge of what had become of Michael. He did not look forward to telling his father he had been so deceived by his own brother.

Feelings he had not felt in centuries were boiling to the forefront of his mind. He wanted to confront him and demand to know the meaning of his still existing and why he ran off from his father. Tell him how he had almost destroyed his father with his disappearance. Demand to know how he could go all this time and not ever reach out to him. Were his feelings for them just a farce? However, he had that damn human with him and he could not just run to the house and break the door down.

A rage he had never felt was taking over and he had to take a moment to get himself under control. When he was calm enough, he looked up at the house and watched what was going on, with a wonder as to what the hell was going on.

Bonaventura watched through the windows while Franco scrambled around the house stuffing a duffel bag with can goods and warm clothing for Bonds. He tossed the man a pair of snow boots and a heavy coat. "You'll be wanting these when we get to the cabin." He told him swinging the bag over his shoulder. He motioned Bonds out the door.

Franco tossed the bag in the trunk. The trunk dropped shut. He received an Earth-shattering jolt to his brain that took him to his knees holding his temples.

Bonaventura was sitting on the edge of his porch leaning forward, his elbows resting on his knees and his fingers clasped together under his chin. He cocked one eyebrow and curved his lips into a slight smile. Jumping to his feet, waving a finger in the air at Franco he swaggered over to the back of the Nova. "Oh, my, my, uncle. What have we here?"

"Get in the car." Franco ordered Bonds. Struggling he pulled himself to his feet holding onto the car bumper. The older man didn't hesitate. He jumped in the passenger side locking the doors behind him. "Well, well, if it isn't little bonnie boy," Franco moaned, "If I had any doubts before..." His breathing was labored as he fought against Bonaventura's unique ability to cause blinding pain inside his head. "...I now know for sure it is your bitch of a sister wreaking havoc once more. Get out of my head you little shit." He yelled, holding his open hands against his head. "Daddy sent you to clean up after her? Or are you planning to rip her throat out like he should have done centuries ago?" He took a step back as he groaned and gasped for a deep breath.

In a flash, Bonaventura was between Franco and the Nova. "I don't want to talk about Selena just yet." He tilted his head from side to side, a heavy breath rolling from his chest in low growling tones. "Where have you been for all these years, uncle? Answer me Michael." He leaned his head back a bit to meet the taller man's gaze. "How could you let father think—no, how could you let *me* think you were dead?" His eyes glazed over as his words turned into full blown snarling growls. "We grieved for you for years. Hell, by the gods' blood, he still grieves for you daily." He got so close in Franco's face they were sharing the same breath. With his voice deepened even more, he spoke deliberately, emphasizing each word, "He nearly wiped out his kind trying to find out what happened to you." He took a long step backward, drew his fist back and sent Franco flying several feet in the air with a quick uppercut that landed him square under the jaw. "You fucking bastard."

Bonaventura came after him with fangs dropped and eyes glowing red. He grabbed him up off the ground by his coat collar. "I will destroy you myself," he belted out slamming him against the trunk of a large live oak.

Franco was not resisting, at least not with any real strength. He looked at the boy who once thought he hung the moon; an unforgiving pain of regret filled Bonaventura's eyes.

Bonaventura looked away when he caught his gaze. Realizing that Franco no longer possessed the strength to fight him, he let him drop to the ground and stood staring at him with bloody tears streaking his face. He was pissed off beyond reason at him, but what he felt most was hurt. Knowing Michael had chosen to leave him alone in his darkness was unbearable. The truth was he would never cause him physical harm, no matter how harshly his anger raged. "What has become of you my uncle?" He offered his hand, helping Franco to his feet.

Franco got up. Brushing himself off he retorted, "Don't call me uncle. We share no blood. I am not your uncle. Vettorio is not my brother. The brother I walked

207

the Earth with side by side before there was man on Earth is no longer. He died when he made the choice of following Lilith and Baldassare into hell," he lied.

"Oh, for the love of Odin get over yourself. You know you are brothers on Earth as you were in Asgard." Bonaventura paced around mocking the words he had heard his father utter so many times. He continued in a somber tone, "You were never far from him. Even in his darkest years, you watched over him. You were all he had left of his previous existence. It nearly destroyed him and me as well, you disappearing like that. You and he are two sides of the same coin. No matter how fucking self-righteous you think you are. You are brothers, equals. At least you were. What the fuck happened to you?" He thought for a second then answered his own question following him toward the porch. Grabbing Franco by the arm, he spun him around to face him. "Holy fucking hell, you look older and you're weak as shit. You have fallen," he smirked, "the great almighty Archangel Michael is but a mere mortal." He scratched his head and smiled. "You know

Selena is going to kick your ass before she rips you to shreds?"

They walked onto the porch and took a seat next to each other. Franco's chest was heaving as he struggled to catch his breath.

"What's with the old guy peeking over the seat there?" Bonaventura laughed pointing to Bonds who drew himself down onto the floor out of sight when he made eye contact with him.

Franco shook his head. He had almost forgotten about Bonds. "He saw Selena feed on his friend. I was taking him away for safe keeping." He wiped the blood off his lower lip with his sleeve. "You still carry quite a punch there, junior." He arched a brow.

"And you hit like a girl. A human one at that," he pushed Franco to the side slightly with his hand against his shoulder. Franco raised his arms to catch his balance. Bonaventura saw the wedding band he still wore. "Is that what happened to you Michael?" He asked catching hold of his hand in midair.

209

Franco pulled his hand free. Twisting his ring around on his finger, he closed his eyes with thoughts of Maria filling his mind for a moment before he answered. "She was my greatest find in this world."

"Was?" Bonaventura questioned.

"She was killed nearly six years ago now," he crossed his ankles and began swinging his feet slightly off the porch. "Some drunk was on his way home from a party just when Maria was headed to work. He ran a traffic light and she was gone. Right there on the spot in the blink of an eye. A bottle of booze and two lives are ended," he jumped up from the porch. "Let's go inside and talk about Selena," he changed the subject.

Franco coaxed Bonds from the car and the three of them went in the house. Franco made a pot of coffee. Bonds stayed in the kitchen while he and Bonaventura went in the living room.

"So what's it like, being human?" Bonaventura sat on the sofa and stretched his long legs out, crossing his ankles. He rested his elbows on his knees; he sipped his coffee and leaned in closer to Franco. He waited like a

210

little kid with baited breath for him to tell all. His anger and momentary hatred had dissipated and he, at that moment just wanted to hear what had been happening with his oldest, hell the only real friend he had ever known.

He had grieved the loss of Michael from his life. It was the only genuine sense of loss he had ever known. He had ached for the times they had talked for hours, alone up in the Alps. Michael was the one who held him most through the pain of his transformation from a normal human into the immortal semi-vampire anomaly he became. Michael had been the only one Bonaventura confided in about how much it tortured him to be a vampire, although he had no real blood lust as other vampires. He did have to learn to hunt and feed on occasion, no matter how repulsive he found it. Finding his own way would have been unbearable without Michael. "Come on, I want to hear."

Franco stuck a cushion behind him leaning back against the sofa arm. "You have always been such an incorrigible little waif." He smiled sipping his coffee.

"You are the one thing I have missed since giving up who I was before," his eyes brightened.

"Now that she's gone do you regret falling? Was she worth it?" Bonaventura questioned.

"Regret, not for a minute and yes, she was more than worth it. Maria was the most unbelievably beautiful human being you could ever imagine. She had the kindest most generous heart." Franco swallowed hard forcing back the lump forming deep in his throat. "I would do it over again in a heartbeat."

Bonaventura cleared his throat "You know I have got to tell him."

"I know, but not tonight kid." Franco patted Bonaventura on the knee as he got up from the sofa. "You can call Vettorio tomorrow. I need to get Bonds out of here." He dug his cell phone out of his pocket and passed it to him. "Put your number in my phone and mine in yours. I'll call you first thing in the morning and we'll go from there." He went to get Bonds from the kitchen.

Getting Bonds settled back into the car and after shutting the door, Franco leaned against the car and let out the longest sigh he'd ever let out, in his long existence. How was he to face Vettorio? He knew the way he left was inexcusable. Nevertheless, he felt it was the only way he could leave at the time. Now he had to explain himself to his longest and dearest friend. Explain how he became a Fallen Angel and what he had been doing with his life, while Vettorio and Bonaventura had been grieving him. He was plagued with so much guilt at learning what his disappearance did to his brother and his brother's son. He knew they would feel his loss, but he did not think he they would grieve as they had and as Vettorio still was. Shaking his head, he cleared his mind and put it back on the task at hand. Vettorio would have to wait, but he knew he would not be able to wait for long.

8

Unicorns are Real

IT WAS 6:30 PM WHEN BONAVENTURA PULLED UP AT CRYSTAL'S HOUSE. Charlie came running around the porch barking and jumping up on him. They were playing tug of war with a chew toy when Crystal opened the door. "Y'all come in out of the cold." The three of them went inside. "I was about to give up on you."

"I'm sorry. My meetings ran way too long and I couldn't slip off." He did not want to lie to her, but it

214

had to be, at least for now. He looked around the room. Crystal had set up a very romantic dinner table in front of the fire complete with flowers and candles. "This is very nice." He took off his coat leaving it on a small wooden bench inside the front door. "I know I'm a bit late, but can I help you with anything?" He followed her to the kitchen.

"Nope, I've got this." She shooed him out of the kitchen, following him with their plates she had kept warm in the oven. "I made Chicken Marsala. It's my first time so I hope it's fit to eat. If not we'll have to go straight for dessert," she laughed.

They ate quietly in front of the fire staring at one another and exchanging small smiles.

Crystal broke the silence. "So Vent, what kind of business are you in?"

"Antiquities, mostly European, but some Middle Eastern stuff." He dabbed at the corners of his mouth with his napkin. Refilling their wine glasses he continued, "My family owns a shop in Baden-Baden as well as Bozen and Milan, Italia."

"I'm impressed." she raised her glass to him.

"There is nothing impressive about it. We just buy and sell old furniture and oil paintings, no big deal."

He flashed her a little boy grin that along with his accent brought Franco to mind. She quickly pushed the thought of him away and tried to focus on those beautiful lips speaking across from her. She surmised he was the most perfect physical specimen of male beauty. He was not as tall as Franco, but muscular.

"When my business is finished perhaps you will come with me. I have an apartment in Milan or maybe we could spend Christmas in Paris."

She smiled really big at Vent while silently screaming *calm the fuck down* to her brain. "Wow. Christmas in Paris and it's just two weeks away. But I couldn't go. I'll be just getting back to work." She stood and started clearing the table.

Taking the plates from her and putting them back down on the table; he took her face in his hands. She tiptoed up to meet his mouth. Bonaventura pulled away to look into her eyes. "You are the most exquisite creature I have ever looked upon." He whispered against her lips before reclaiming their kiss. The kiss was long and deep.

Vent carried her off to the bed tossing her playfully. He took hold of her ankles lifting them midair shaking her jeans until they were off and on the floor. Raising his eyebrows, he did a little strip tease that got Crystal tickled and she could not help but start giggling. "Not the reaction I was going for my dear," he snatched her by her feet to the edge of the bed nibbling at her toes working up the insides of her legs slowly with kisses. He lingered in places that he deduced would excite her a bit more. He loved the way she would squirm and could not help but enjoy holding her in place. He slowly made it to his destination and took a long, slow taste. "You taste like sunshine." He moaned exploring her tender folds with his tongue. Sliding two fingers inside of her warm cavity, he felt Crystal twist her hips and arch her back pulling him deeper into her mound with her hands braced on either side of his head. He brought her to a screaming climax before backing off. He stood up smiling.

Crystal sat up on the edge of the bed. Taking his steely shaft in one hand, she began slowly tracing its full length with her tongue. He groaned loudly, the speed of her mouth was met by the thrust of his hips. Crystal slowly took him in fully and slowly back out, dragging her teeth. She smiled as he looked down at her with wide eyes. She knew exactly what she was doing and she loved it. Just as she thought he was about to climax she gingerly slipped her index finger inside of him adding to the intensity of his pleasure.

"For the love of Odin." He cried out before collapsing to his knees. Pushing her back against the bed, he placed a tender kiss at her belly button, letting his body go limp on hers, the side of his face against her stomach.

"What did you say? Odin?" Crystal ran her fingers through his hair.

"Yes, I suppose I did." He let out a tiny chuckle between blowing breaths. "I've been reading about

218

Norse mythology. That just popped in my head." He covered his slip. "Round two coming up shortly," crawling his way back on to the bed. Straddling her, he pinned her wrists to the bed over her head. He started kissing one shoulder working his way across her collarbone and up her neck to that little spot that made her dance beneath him. He stretched out working his legs between hers. He let out a slight growl forcing his fangs to retract. He ran his tongue across his teeth. Licking his lips, he continued nibbling her sweet spot, as she called it, on her neck just beneath her ear. Bonaventura worked his way down ever inch of her ivory skin devouring her until she buried her nails into his back and moaned out in supplication for him to enter her. He smiled pleased with her begging for him. He reclaimed her mouth, kissing her deeply, making her taste herself as he slid inside of her.

In a flash, he had flipped her over on all fours, his steely manhood ready to claim her completely. He reached around her tiny frame with one arm so that he could fondle her tender folds between his fingers.

Crystal rocked her hips back against his thighs to match his rhythm. She let out a climactic cry. Bonaventura leaned in wrapping his arms around her tighter.

"Oh gods, Crystal, are you ready? I don't know how gentle I can be right now."

She moaned and rocked her hips again as she continued to try to catch her breath after the intense orgasm.

He knew he could not hold back, he pushed himself fully inside of her thrusting in and out pushing her over the edge. Each thrust was a new feeling for each of them and neither of them could hold out much longer. They both reached their climax at the same time, groaning loudly in unison. Crystal fell into a heap against the bed totally spent.

Vent slowly crawled up next to her, actually finding he needed to breathe hard. It was such a strange sensation for him, one that had never happened before. He would think on that, but it would have to wait for a bit. He had a beautiful woman to attend to. Propping up on one elbow, he ran his index finger around the outline of the unicorn tattoo that covered her right shoulder. "What if I told you I could take you to a place where they still exist?" He whispered kissing her shoulder.

Crystal rolled over on her side to face him. "I beg your pardon? What still exists?" She locked her eyes onto his lips curving in a tense smile.

"Unicorns," he answered. "If another realm existed where such things were not myth, would you travel there with me?" He felt a nervous stammer take control of his tongue.

She looked at him as if he was joking and started laughing. She was laughing so hard he thought for sure she was about to turn purple. Then she noticed he was not laughing along with her. Her smile fell and she became noticeably agitated.

"Really? I knew you were too good to be true. What the fuck have you been smoking?" She let out a nervous laugh as she gathered the sheet around her getting out of the bed.

He followed after her. "Crystal, wait! I wanted to wait until the right time to tell you everything, but events beyond my control have forced me to expedite matters. I am sorry, but we must talk about this." He caught her by the arm spinning her around to face him. The look in his eyes told her he wasn't kidding around.

"This is unfucking believable," she shook her head. "We just had the fuck of a lifetime and now you want to talk about other realms and shit. What the hell, Vent?" She pulled her arm free. "Don't. You don't have to pretend to be crazy as an out. Just say so and walk away. I'm a big girl I can handle it." She made her way back to the room and hurriedly put her clothes on.

Vent did the same then flashed in front of her cutting her off at the doorway. "There are many things I can tell you for certain, but this even surprises me. I do not know what has come over me, I have never felt this way, but knowing what I know about myself, means I do understand this is real. It will not make sense to you and believe me; I wish I had a better way to tell you what I am about to tell you. There are things you do not know even exist. Nevertheless, I find I must tell you about them because of one simple fact. I am in love with you Crystal and you have no idea how very long I have waited to say those words," bloody tears began to pool in his eyes.

"Oh. My. God." Crystal touched her hand to his face "Vent what's wrong with you? We need to get you to the hospital." Her outrage was stilled by concern.

"It is nothing." He cut her off taking her hand in his. "I'm trying to tell you who, what I am. Will you please sit down and listen?" She nodded in agreement, but he could see the hesitation was back strong and her cop mind was already trying to make sense of this by using several certain scenarios. He loved that about her mind. He would need her help when it came to Selena, it was helpful to know she had such an active mind that might be able to help him get ahead of his sister.

Leading her back into the room, they took a seat at the foot of her bed. He held both of her hands inside one of his and again found his mind wandering. Her hands were so small compared to his. What if he could

223

not protect her from what he was about to tell her? So many things could happen after his truth came out. She could be a target for Selena. If she ever found out he loved this human, Selena would do her best to get her and torture her. This made him hesitate a moment. Did he really want to burden her with this secret and in essence threaten her life? He knew he could not live without her, even after only knowing her the very short time he had. Either way, Selena could find out about her and use Crystal against him. It was best she knew everything she could, and know he would protect her with his very being. He noticed she was growing restless while he was mulling over his thoughts.

"There are people in this world that are unlike any you have known. All myths come from ancient truths and legends." He took a deep breath. "Thousands of years ago, before there were humans there was a great disruption in the heavens. The first woman made by the gods became very defiant. She thought herself equal to the gods. As punishment, she along with two angels that followed her, were banished and cursed, each to their own hell." He shifted nervously.

She stood up, and walked to the doorway. Turning to face him, she leaned against the doorframe. "Is this going to be a lesson on mythology? I know the basics, but go ahead. I'm listening." Crystal did not understand why but she found herself hanging on his every word even though she had begun to question his sanity and her own for standing there. Part of her wanted to believe him, but the detective in her was afraid he was fucking Looney Tunes and she was getting in a position to get the hell out of there.

Vent slid as close to the end of the bed as he could without falling off. He rested his forearms against his knees. Looking up at her, "I swear to you I am not crazed. What I am is an anomaly. Even in a world of extreme beings, I am different from the others." Washing a hand down his face, he hesitated.

"Just fucking spit it out already. Don't clam up now. Just go with it, all the way through, nonstop. I think I can handle it better that way." She spouted off the words with a sharp tongue.

"Very well then." He stood. "I was born in the year 0818. I guess you could say I am an odd hybrid of sorts. I have a beating heart, fully functioning lungs, but I am an immortal. I have not aged a day since I turned twenty-five. Although, a stake can destroy me, it must be made from the world tree, Yggdrasil. I can walk in daylight, as can only a few. My mother was pregnant with me when she fell in love with my true father, the king of the vampire nation. That is a story I must share with you at another time. Their union made me what I am." He looked away breaking their eye contact for a few seconds before turning back to her. "I am a vampire, Crystal. I do not sparkle in the sun or glow in the dark. I do not go around attacking humans in the night or turn into a fucking bat. On occasion, my eyes do glow red if I am angry, or overly aroused. I do not sleep in a coffin, but I do on occasion sleep. My beating heart allows me to go long periods without consuming blood. I tend to feed on animals. I much prefer a rib eye steak."

226

He smirked in an attempt to lighten the mood. "Extra garlic."

Crystal started laughing and could not stop herself. She found herself back on the bed doubled over. There was a small part of her brain screaming at her to get the fuck out of there. She was a fool to go back into the room with him. Tears were streaming down her face when she regained control of herself and she felt the anger consume her.

"Prove it! Show me," she demanded.

Bonaventura willed his fangs to drop and his eyes glowed red.

Crystal screamed running for the front door. He flashed between her and the door. "How the fuck do you do that?" She pounded her fists against his chest. He stood still and let her unleash her frustration for a couple of minutes before catching her gently by the wrists.

"I am no monster, Crystal." He forced her right hand open placing it against his chest and holding it there under his hand. "Feel my warm skin, my beating heart? What we have only comes around once if you are lucky and I have waited nearly twelve hundred years for you. I want to spend eternity with you Crystal, to show you worlds you never imagined, but most of all I want to hold you in my arms and know you love me the way I do you." He tilted her face up to his with a finger curled under her chin.

Crystal was caught in his gaze; she could see there was truth in his words reflecting in his dark eyes that had gone back to normal. Losing all resolve, she pulled her hands free and snaked her arms around his neck crying. "I am not sure how we're going to pull this shit off, but I don't want to lose this feeling you've stirred in me. I, too, know I care for you deeply. The cop in me cannot explain it and certainly cannot justify it. I know better than this, but I cannot escape it. You are either one crazy ass bastard, or you truly are what you say you are. I cannot imagine you are able to fake those eyes and those teeth. I do not know why I am in your arms right now. Maybe I'm a bit sadistic, but I can't walk away from you."

A sigh of relief escaped from deep within Bonaventura. Before he could respond to her words, his entire body quaked so hard it shook both of them to the core. He stretched his full height sniffing the air. Selena was near. Crystal gasped as she watched his eyes begin to glow again; the blood veins around his eyes came to the surface pulsating to a dark purple. He covered her mouth with his hand shaking his head no. Mouthing his words to her silently, "If you never do anything you are told again, please do as I ask now or we both are dead." His facial expression screamed volumes to her and she nodded in agreement.

Charlie whimpered from his spot on the blanket. Bonaventura patted his hand against his leg twice. Charlie came to him and he glamoured the lab to insure his silence. In a flash, he scooped them both up and set them down in the attic. He kissed Crystal and whispered softly against her ear. "Do not come down stairs no matter what you hear, please."

229

Crystal nodded in acknowledgment. Cupping his face in her hands she mouthed the words, "You better be okay down there, I love you."

Bonaventura nodded and winked. Then he was gone.

Sitting down on the floor, she cradled Charlie in her arms. Hiding out was against her nature but her every instinct was telling her this was not the time to stand her ground. She wished she had her gun, but something told her it would not save her if she found the need to use it.

When he flashed back to the living room Bonaventura sent a quick text to Franco. "Uncle, Selena is here at Crystal Harley's house come now." He dropped his cell back in his jeans pocket and picked up his jacket from the bench near the front door. From an inside pocket, he removed two slender wooden stakes made from a branch of Yggdrasil. They were each eight inches long and sharpened to a fine point on either end.

He walked outside. Stepping softly, he followed the wrap around porch to the back. The moon shone bright illuminating the area between the house and the crashing waves of the Atlantic. The crisp winter air carried the pungent salty aroma of the nearby marsh assaulting Bonaventura's ultra-sense of smell once again.

He hoped Michael got his text and was able to get here quickly. If Selena was here, she had to have overheard part of what he told Crystal and that was not going to be good for either of them. He knew he needed help in protecting her. Selena was vicious and she may not be alone. He made sure to keep his emotions hidden, as he did not need his sister having any other advantages over him. He felt like this might be the fight of his life. His soul mate was going to need him to protect her from this evil and he was going to make damned sure he did.

9

Not All Sisters Are Created Equal

SELENA WAS STANDING LESS THAN A HUNDRED FEET IN FRONT OF HIM. The ocean breeze was blowing her long hair lightly around her shoulders. She smiled wickedly, watching Bonaventura come down the steps toward her. His eyes locked on hers, he was totally focused on Selena, so focused he failed to notice she was not alone. The wooden arrow of the crossbow ripped through his back then his heart and half way back out of his chest. Blood was spurting from the wound. He growled loudly in pain. Falling to his knees, he released the stakes held in his hands to pull the arrow the rest of the way through and free from his body.

Selena flashed to him. Picking up the two pieces of wood, she smirked. "Not so tough now are you little prince?" The arrow could not kill him, but it certainly weakened him long enough to allow her to sadistically toy with him, as she liked. Selena wasted no time in taking him to the ground before he could come back from the blow of the arrow that ripped through him. Straddling him at his waist, she used his stakes to pin him down, one through each hand into the ground. His body wrenched in pain and he could not get inside of her mind. The wood of Yggdrasil had struck him powerless. Selena rose up hovering over him on all fours. Leaning down close, she broke into song, "Have you any idea how I have longed for this moment, this moment, any idea, idea, idea?" She grinned wide, baring her fangs. She got close to him again and took a long pull of air into her lungs. She smiled evilly. "Oh brother of mine, how delightful of you to make this so much more enjoyable for me. Did you enjoy her like you have enjoyed the others? Of course you did. You are like me aren't you?"

Vent arched his back and growled at her comment. "I am nothing like you." The look of pure hatred was tinted with a bit of fear he held in his heart that she would know what Crystal was to him. He had to play her down so Selena would never know. "But you are right sister, she was just a fuck. You caught me with my pants down. Now why don't we move this elsewhere so that little human doesn't see anything she doesn't need to see?"

"Why would I care if she saw? I am not above killing, as you know. Maybe I am getting tired of killing men and a female you have just enjoyed would be a nice change to my palate." She smiled with a look that just screamed insanity. He had to get her away from this house, but at the same time, need to make sure Michael was here to protect Crystal. But how would that happen? Michael would attack Selena as soon as he saw her and vice versa. Vent's only hope was that Michael would think sensibly, stand back, and get to Crystal without Selena noticing. Vent had to keep her full attention.

"You know I cannot let you harm the human. You have to know this is why I am here. I am to stop you. You have to stop this. But know this, he will hunt you down and destroy you for killing me." Bonaventura yelled out.

"Oh, but I do not intend to kill you, my dear." She let out a hideous laugh from deep in her belly. "Not just yet anyway. But that little creature you have hiding in there," She nodded toward the house, "I smell the stench of her ripe little human juices all over you. I shall take great pleasure in watching you as I slowly disassemble her fragile body and feed her bones to the hounds of hell." She pressed her right hand hard against his mouth in muzzle fashion and bit down on her index finger of the other hand rolling her eyes up in thought. "Yes, perhaps drawn and quartered would befit her, as your future would be... never shall be...mate. I have seen firsthand the pain of such a death is absolutely unimaginable." Her entire face lit up with the idea. "I can fashion you a necklace of her entrails." She let go of his mouth to clap her hands in self-praise of her idea.

"Selena, I swear by the god's blood if you touch her. I will hunt you down and end you." He bucked in a lost effort to toss her away. She pulled her knees tight against his waist, waggling a finger in his face before kissing the tip of his nose. He spat at her.

She cupped a hand under his chin squeezing his lips together with one hand while she dug her fingernails into the soft flesh of his neck with her free hand then licked his blood from her fingernails. She giggled with glee, "Oh dear brother! I knew I was right! She is your soul mate. How sweet that you have found what daddy and mommy have. I thought this day would never come. I shall have to throw you a party after I kill her." Putting her finger to the side of her mouth," But you might be a downer at that point. So I shall throw you both a party, celebrating your love and then kill her at the climax of it all."

He could feel her accomplice approaching even before he heard Crystal's voice. "Take your hands off of me you son-of-a-bitch." She was struggling in vain to free her arm from his clutches

Looking up, he made eye contact with him. Bonaventura sucked in a deep breath in disbelief. "You? What the hell? Why?" He let his eyes travel back and forth from him to Crystal.

Baldassare towered over him smirking. The thousands of years of living in darkness with Lilith did not show on his flawless angelic face. Like Vettorio, he maintained the soft features of an angel. He was tall and lean with chestnut colored eyes, hair hanging around his shoulders. "I have waited patiently for an opportunity to show your beloved father how I feel about him." He squatted down resting his haunches on the back of his heels forcing Crystal to her knees. He tenderly let the back of his free hand glide down the side of Selena's face. "Finding your sister and seeing that she felt the same as I did, was such a great end to my dull days. The bonus was how amazing a fuck she is and how we never seem to tire of each other. She brings me much joy and it brings us both delight knowing your pussy of a father, loathes how we lead our lives. Or should I say, her life, as he knows nothing of my involvement. My Selena will decide whether you are allowed to tell him about my involvement. I sure hope she does, as I would love to cause him more anguish. He is undeserving and it is time he knows the truth of it. The beginning of your end starts with your human." Grabbing her by the back of her head, his fist full of her hair, he shoved Crystal's face nose to nose with Bonaventura. A deep evil laugh erupted from his chest. He released his hold and came to his feet.

Bonaventura looked at Crystal, his eyes filled with love and fear. "I am so sorry." His words were choppy. The blood building up inside of him formed tiny coppery bubbles on his lips with each word he coughed out. The lethal properties of the stakes were pumping their deadly toxins into his veins and preventing his body from healing itself.

Crystal put her hand to his chest in an attempt to slow the bleeding. "Shush. Don't try to speak. Save your breath baby." With every beat of his heart the blood pumped between her fingers, flowing across her hand. "Why are you doing this?" She turned her head to face Selena. "Get the fuck off of him bitch."

Selena only smiled and dug her knees tighter beneath his rib cage before slamming the back of her hand across Crystal's cheek sending her flat against the frozen ground. "You fucking slut!"

Crystal pushed up off the ground and came at Selena only to be knocked down again, this time drawing blood beneath her left eye. Baldassare lifted her to her feet by her hair, holding her back from going at Selena again.

Selena looked at Baldassare with an amused grin. "She has a pair, I'll give her that." Returning her attention to Bonaventura Selena dug her finger in the hole left by the arrow twisting it deep and reveling in the obvious pain she was inflicting.

239

Franco had just pulled onto highway 17 when the text from Bonaventura came through. "What the hell?" He rolled the window down, stuck the police siren on the roof of the Nova and spun around in the highway.

Bonds just looked on in terror. In the couple of days since he had met Franco, he quickly learned to keep his mouth shut and hang on for a bumpy ride.

The screaming siren was picked up miles away by Selena's keen sense of hearing. "Your little pet is saved for tonight. I am in no mood to have the authorities' bare witness to our family squabble. But rest assured brother. She is not safe, not by any stretch of the imagination." She slapped his face leaving her handprint across his cheek and knocked Crystal to the ground. "I am going to take great joy in watching your slow death little one." She growled at Crystal. In a flash Selena and Baldassare disappeared.

Franco came barreling up to the house in a trail of dust. He sprang from the car and was headed to the front door when he heard Crystal calling out. Following the sound of her voice Franco found them. Bonaventura still staked to the ground ghostly pale in a pool of his own blood. Crystal was struggling in vain to remove the stakes from his hands. "Please help me. I can't pull them out." She pleaded sobbing.

Franco felt his heart drop looking at Bonaventura.

He had nearly bled out from the gaping hole that still spilled his blood with every beat of his heart. He willed his body to force the words from his lungs in a string of gurgled moans, "Baldassare has taken up with Selena. He is seeking revenge against father. If it is not too much ask..." He coughed up more bloody bubbles that rolled out the corner of his mouth leaving a trail down the side of his face. "Do you think you could help us out here?" The small stakes from the World tree held him steadfast to the ground, his upper body immobile. The excruciating pain was pulsing down his arms, radiating sharply through his entire body. It was unlike

241

anything he had ever experienced. He did not want Crystal to know the extent of the pain he was in. It was taking all of his willpower to suppress the screams that were trying to escape his throat.

Franco stepped one foot over Bonaventura's chest. Straddling him he leaned over, taking hold of a stake and pulling as hard as he could. However, as a mortal he did not possess the power to so much as move the stake free from the ground. He looked at Bonaventura, his eyes filled with empathy. "This is going to hurt like pure hell kid." He went to his knees next to one stake and then the other. Using every ounce of strength he had, he slowly and with great care rocked and tugged until both hands were freed.

Bonaventura let go a series of feral screams as his flesh tore from around the pieces of wood.

"Jesus Christ kid, you're a mess." He helped him to his feet. "You need to feed and soon." Bonaventura nodded weakly in agreement looking down at the amount of his blood pooled against the frozen ground. "You should begin to heal now that the stakes have been removed." Franco lifted Bonaventura's arm up across his shoulder. Crystal quickly took the other arm and they walked him into the house. They sat Bonaventura on the bench inside the door.

"Oh dear God Vent." Crystal went to her knees in front of him. "Please be alright." She placed open hands on either side of his face.

"I will be fine in just a short time," he offered up a weak smile.

"Qualcuno aveva meglio iniziare a spiegare cosa diavolo sta succedendo qui." Franco shook his head, repeating himself for Crystal's benefit. "Someone had better start explaining what the hell is going on here." He snorted, a pained look of confusion spreading across his face.

Crystal looked up at him. "How did you even know to come here, DeLuca?" She darted one of her *what the fuck* looks at him. She started to get frantic, which was unlike her. She was always known for keeping her head, but she found she could not in this situation. This was not good. She was trying to control herself, but found it more and more difficult to do.

"Junior called me," he walked over to the liquor cabinet, took out a bottle of whiskey and brought it back tipping the bottle to Bonaventura's lips. "Drink this." He sat down on the bench next to him. Taking a pull from the bottle after him. Franco gave them both an inquiring stare. "One of you can start talking any time now."

"Stop the damn bus a minute." Crystal came to her feet snatching the bottle. "How do you two know each other?" She turned the bottle up gulping it down before Franco could take it back from her.

"Look here princess. Getting drunk on your ass is not going to provide the answers either of us seeks." Franco scorned.

"I followed her here from the station. I had no idea you were in love with her." Bonaventura spoke, his words trailing off to a whimper.

"You did what?" Crystal growled through clenched teeth stomping her foot. Her fear was fast being overtaken by anger. "You've been playing me? And he is no such thing." Her eyes were darting back and forth between the two men.

"Yes, it is true, I was following you but no game playing, you have my word. And he does love you. I am not mistaken. I saw it in his eyes when he didn't know it was my blood all over you." He glanced over at Franco, who was looking at the floor then back to Crystal. "He and I have known each other for a very long time. I will explain everything to you soon. I swear it. But first we must prepare for Selena's return."

Franco took off his coat. Pushing his shirtsleeve up, he held his arm out in front of Bonaventura. "Take it." He could see his reluctance to feed in front of Crystal. "Princess, there is a man out in the Nova. I am sure you will find him cowering in the floor scared half to death. Would you please go coax him out and bring him in the house?" He turned his head to Crystal winking at her. "And take your time if you would *il mio amore.*"

Crystal did as he asked without saying anything. She could sense the importance of leaving them alone. She walked around Franco and kissed Vent on the top of his head before going out the door. She saw the man peeking over the door in the car. She grumbled to herself and thought he could just cool his jets in there for a bit longer.

There was an intense pressure at her temples and she started to massage them, in hopes of making it go away. It did seem to work, but her mind was still flooded with everything that seemed to have just happened within minutes. Her life would never be the same, for that she was sure. She had so many questions, but first, she needed to know what the connection with Franco and Vent was. She was a good bullshit detector, so she would know if either of them was lying to her. But after what Vent just told her about himself, she couldn't even begin to fathom what Franco had to say about his part in all of this. Shaking her head, she started down the steps to the Nova, to fetch Bonds and bring him into the kitchen from the back of the house.

Bonaventura took Franco's arm in his hand, "Are you sure about this? I am all but drained. I fear I may not be able to stop myself once the flow begins," his eyes filled with apprehension. "And without your grace to heal you I am…"

"You'll stop kid. I have faith." He interrupted turning his head away.

Bonaventura's elongated fangs pierced into the tender flesh of Franco's forearm. The warm coppery taste rolled across his tongue, the flavor bursting inside his mouth as the sweet nectar began to flow down the back of his throat forcing his eyes closed by the euphoric sensation he had not allowed himself in more than a decade. The harder he pulled, the hungrier he became. Almost succumbing to blood lust he barely heard his name being called.

"Vent! Stop! You're going to kill him." Crystal cried out when she came back in the room seeing how pale Franco had become. She went to them and placed a hand on either side of his face against Franco's arm. "Baby, please let him go. You can do this." She pleaded.

247

She hoped she could reach him. This was so far from her realm of reality that she could hardly believe she was trying to talk a vampire down from taking another hit of his drug. She could feel the tension release bit by bit in his body and she hoped this was a good thing. It had to be, right?

Bonaventura opened his eyes looking up at her. He slowly retracted his fangs and let go. "I never wanted..."

"I know," she cut him off, "it's going to be all right." Crystal cradled his head lovingly in her arms. When she turned around Franco was gone.

"Vent, I have to go find him. He had to have lost a lot of blood. He looked so pale, I can't even imagine he was able to get up and leave."

Bonaventura held her in place, feeling his strength coming back to him. "He will be okay. He needs time to process everything that has just happened. This will all be explained to you, I promise, but his past life just smacked him in the face and he is going to need some time."

Bonaventura hoped what he was telling her was the truth. In fact, he had no idea if he would find him again. It wasn't like he hadn't disappeared on them before. He knew he needed to tell Crystal everything, but right now, he felt still out of sorts and needed more time. Thankfully, she was quiet and processing everything herself. He needed to gather his thoughts so he could explain things thoroughly and precisely, in a way that she would understand. Many humans didn't know much at all about the gods and what they did know, they believed to be fables. Her life had just been turned upside down and he needed to make sure to right it for her again, with him by her side.

Crystal had Bonds picked up and taken to a safe house after Bonaventura glamoured him to forget the events he had witnessed, including seeing Selena before at the pier.

10

Wings Gifted From Thor

AS THE SEA GAVE BIRTH TO THE RISING SUN

IN THE DISTANCE, Franco sat on the rocks staring

into the waves tumbling against the sand. The cold

winter air nipped at his face. The beach was his favorite

place to think, to be as one with nature. He had not

stepped foot inside of a church or even prayed since the

day he cursed the gods for taking Maria away from him,

six years ago.

He dropped his jacket on the rocks. Walking to the edge of the surf, he prayed to whoever might still listen to him, "Father's, please prepare me for this journey you have set before me. I do not understand why you have allowed this to come about. Have you forsaken me as I had you? Is this the start of my tribulation to prove I am still worthy?" Tears began to well up in his eyes. "*Padre mi perdoni per quello che può venire.* (Father, forgive me for what may come.) I ask your forgiveness for the wrongs I have committed against you now, for I do not wish to perish without the opportunity to atone for my sins against you all."

He dug Maria's rosary from his pocket. Hanging it around his neck, he kissed it and looked to the quickly darkening sky. "My darling, I miss you so very badly," he wiped at the tears streaking down his face. "Watch over our sweet Isabella. I fear I am not fated to survive this trial."

Franco fell to his knees in the freezing cold surf praying to the gods. The waves grew fierce pounding against the sand, white foam engulfing him to his waist.

251

The blackened sky filled with lightning strikes that reached down, licking at the sea. A smile tugged at his lips with the knowledge that Thor was listening to his pleas. "Father, I beg of you to return me to that which I was, what I gave up of my own free will. I shall not regret my love of Maria and my Isabella is everything to me, but I must do this. You know this battle against the darkness is mine to finish in your names. I cannot defeat her alone. Please allow me to do your bidding, mighty Thor. I must put an end to her plague against humanity. Walk by my side once again mighty god that you might guide my hands as your own."

The surf slowly began to calm, receding from around him. Franco banged his open hands against the sand. Digging his fingers into the ground, he pulled his fists tight around wet sand. His anguished body wrenched into a fetal position. He could not suppress the screams building up from the pain. With one feral scream after another for over an hour, he felt himself regressing. He struggled to his feet ripping away his shirt. Pawing at the skin over his shoulder blades where he felt the blood begin to run down his back. The wings he had given up fourteen years ago were tearing their way free from beneath his flesh. Every inch brought more pain until in one final cry he held his open hands to the sky and his wings unfurled into their glorious splendor.

"Thank you, *padre*." He wept more profusely. Lowering his hands slowly, he willed his wings to tuck back into their hiding place where the angel wing tattoo had been carried on his back since he had fallen. It was now gone. Franco let out a sigh of relief; a half smile graced his lips. Walking back toward the rocks where he had left his leather jacket, he saw Crystal.

She came sprinting down the beach almost running into Franco before she came to a stop. She grabbed hold of his arms. Her chest was heaving. She was breathless. It was hard to get the words out, "I thought you would be here. Have you lost your freaking mind? How could you just disappear on me?" She pulled him close wrapping her arms around his waist. "You're freezing. I'm so sorry. But I love him Franco. No shit, I am so in love with Vent that it hurts. I don't care what he is," she rattled off without giving him a chance to respond. "I would have been here sooner but I was afraid to leave him. It got pretty bad before he started to heal. Please don't hate me."

"You silly, silly girl. Don't you understand how important you have become to my life? I love you. I will die for you." His words were drawn out and deliberate. Franco took her face in his hands kissing her long and deep. Taking a step back he caught her surprised gaze, "I have thought about doing that for some time now." He smiled. "Our lips will never touch again, just this once, just in case." He hugged her tightly.

"Will die?" She questioned craning her neck against his chest to look up at him. Franco released her, slipping his jacket on without answering. "And how dare you kiss me like that now, now after all this time?"

He took Crystal by the hand leading her back toward the Nova. "Come. Walk with me. There are some truths I must share with you." He pulled her along. "I have loved you for some time now but my life is too complicated. There was the whole working together thing and now junior." He shook his head. "I just wanted you to know, in case..." his words trailed off to a whisper.

Crystal noticed he somehow looked different. There was a calming sense of peace about him that she failed to understand, considering they may all be dead by nightfall. She squeezed his hand tightly. "I am honest to God scared shitless over this whole nightmare. Please tell me we're all going to walk away from this in one piece." She looked at him pleadingly. "Are you like him? Are you a vampire? How could I have no idea?"

Franco pulled her closer draping an arm across her shoulders "No, vampire I am not, princess." He cleared his throat, "I am an..." He hesitated thinking how absurd it was going to sound to her. Stopping, he turned to face her. "Crystal, I am an angel. I have existed since long before mankind. I know this is a lot for you to take in all at one time, but it is important you understand fully all that is about to transpire."

Crystal nodded blinking, "I want you to tell me everything. I can handle it. I mean for Christ's sake a vampire and an angel; can it get any more fucked up?"

"Selena is a dark evil creature. She is a very old and strong vampire. If she is traveling with Baldassare, who is a fallen angel, she will draw on his strength making her more formidable than ever."

"Why does she hate you and Vent so?"

"Let me give you the condensed version. Bonaventura's father, Vettorio and I were once angels together in Asgard, home of the god's. He made some really unfortunate choices that landed him in big trouble. He was made a vampire as punishment. The first ever created. Selena was one of three females he turned, in an effort to make himself a family. She was always evil. Vettorio met and fell in love with Althea and Bonaventura was born. Selena became consumed with jealousy and hatred toward the child and his mother. To her mind they had captured Vettorio's heart and stole him away from her. That hatred has been festering inside her for close to twelve hundred years. As

256

for me, well, she rather had the hots for me, I did not like her back. To further anger her, I stopped her from killing Bonaventura when he was but a boy."

"Holy shit, that's a long time for a bitch to be pissed off. Oh, I'm sorry." It suddenly dawned on her how often she had taken the Lord's name in vain and any number of other choice words she had uttered at him over the years. "I hope you're not offended your holiness." She covered her face with her hand blushing pink.

Franco chuckled. "There is no *your holiness* in this vessel. And yes, it is a very long time to harbor such hatred. Even for an immortal." He opened the car door for her to climb in then went around to the driver's side and got in. "Does the kid know where you are?"

"He was finally sleeping. The healing seems to be slower than he expected. He is still really weak. I left Charlie lying vigilant across his legs on the bed and I put those awful stakes next to him. You don't think she'll come back before tonight do you?"

257

"Not likely. She can walk in the day but she is a creature of the night. She left him in pain and will want him to suffer for some time before she strikes again. I hope that she has no idea just yet that I am here. The element of surprise would certainly favor us. Selena enjoys games more than anyone I have ever known. She will want to play it out before she ends it. She will expect the stakes to hold firm. You would not have been capable of removing them and she knows he would die before allowing you to call for help and expose his true self to others."

"Have you ever gone up against her before?"

"This will be the second time and I have faith it will be the last. I will end her if it takes my last breath."

"Don't talk like that. You are not to die Michael Francis DeLuca. I forbid it."

"Well in that case Miss Harley, I shall do my very best not to die." He tightened his grip around the steering wheel and forced a nervous laugh.

Bonaventura had been pacing the floor worrying about where they were or if Selena had Crystal. He had healed completely save a small tear in each palm from the stakes. He flashed to meet the car when they pulled up to the house. Crystal was out of the car and in her living room safe in his arms before she even saw him coming. "Do you have any idea how worried I have been? When I woke up and you were gone it scared the hell out of me." He kissed her. He looked up at Franco in the doorway. A sudden look of gleeful surprise sprang into his eyes. "Hey, I can feel you again. Why are you all wet?" He beamed.

"Yes, I would imagine you can indeed and I went for a bit of a swim."

"So you're packing feathers again?" His eyes widened.

"Only you would ever refer to my wings as packing feathers." Franco shook his head "Yes, and I am fully loaded with grace as well." He gave thumbs up motion along with a slight laugh.

Bonaventura picked Crystal up spinning around in circles. "We may well live through this shit storm after all."

"That's the plan kid." Franco excused himself to get a hot shower and some dry clothes. Crystal gave him a pair of her sweat pants to wear while his jeans were in the dryer. The legs of her pants fell mid-calf.

Bonaventura could not resist teasing him about the hulk pants. He snickered under his breath. "Love that look you have going on there, angel."

"Ha ha, call your *padre* yet?" He frowned at Bonaventura. Taking Crystal by her hand, he led her to a stool at the kitchen bar. "Now, let's get you something to eat."

Bonaventura took a deep breath and punched Vettorio's number up on his cell. "Father. I have some things we must discuss." He walked to the window looking out at the sleet that had begun again. It was popping off the metal roof in a rhythmic tone.

Vettorio was walking down the sidewalk about to head into their apartment when the phone rang. Catching an unfamiliar tone in his son's voice, he stopped cold. "What is wrong?" He scowled "Is it Selena? What has she done?"

"In part, yes it has to do with her." He chewed nervously at his bottom lip. "I saw her last night. Father, Baldassare is traveling with her."

"That is not possible. He would not dare." Vettorio's tone turned dark and imposing.

"It is true. I saw him myself, father." He hesitated, not sure how much of last night's events he should share over the phone. He did not want to throw his father into a furious panic "He put an arrow through my back last night."

"Are you all right?" Vettorio continued inside the apartment.

"I am well." Bonaventura answered.

Vettorio grabbed his passport and car keys from the side table next to the door along with an overnight bag he had yet to unpack since arriving in Milan. "I am on

261

my way there as we speak. My jet will be waiting and ready to go when I reach the airport. I should be there in approximately ten hours."

"There is more. Michael is here. He is well. I will explain everything when you arrive." His words drifted off to a whisper.

"What do you mean, Michael? How is that possible, my son?" Vettorio felt a range of emotions hit him all at once, shock, anger, confusion and joy. "What the hell is going on?" He demanded.

"I promise a full explanation, but for now please just let it go." He pleaded.

"Very well, I shall hold any further questions until we are face to face. But there had damn well better be a good explanation." Vettorio hung up, got into his Aston Martin and sped off. He called ahead so his private jet would be fueled with their flight plan filed by the time he arrived at the airport.

Bonaventura dropped his cell phone in his pocket then went to the kitchen. "He's on his way, should be here around midnight." He kissed Crystal on the forehead and took a seat on the stool next to her.

Franco flipped the omelet he was making for Crystal from the frying pan onto a plate and placed it in front of her. He leaned back against the cabinet across from Crystal and Bonaventura. Resting his elbows on the counter top behind him, he blew out a breath.

"Before he gets here, I would appreciate some answers myself. So be prepared, you might have to answer them again. I am hoping I might be able to fend off my father from attacking you. You almost killed him, if it were possible, when you left with no notice. Why did you do it? How did you fall? In addition, the one that kills me the most to hear the answer to is how could you stay away from us? From me?" Bonaventura looked up at Michael for the first time since he started asking his questions. Questions he and his father had been asking for a very long time.

Michael looked him in the eyes, "Kid, I know saying I am sorry doesn't make up for the way things turned out. I had been troubled for centuries and I did a selfish thing. I met Maria and she gave me a sense of peace that had been missing from me for so very long. I went to Odin. He granted my wish and allowed me to fall, to live as a human. As to why I have stayed away, I have more than myself to think about." He washed his face in his hands not sure, if he wanted to share any more information about his family. When he looked back up into Bonaventura's questioning gaze, he knew he would tell him everything. "I have a daughter, Isabella. I never wanted her exposed to my past life. She is everything to me and I chose to put her first, as she should be."

Bonaventura let out a shocked gasp, "You have a child, a real flesh and blood child of your own? By the gods that is amazing." His eyes brightened, a wide smile spreading across his lips. "How did the badge come about?"

"My father-in-law is a retired New York City cop. He was my inspiration. I knew I had to do something with my time as a human and what better job for a fallen guardian than to look after others, the whole making things right for the innocent mentality?" He smiled lightly. "Any other questions kid?"

"Just one," Bonaventura gritted his teeth ready to cushion the blow of the answer he was afraid to hear but he wanted, no he had to know for sure "Are you truly in love with Crystal?"

Crystal's eyes bulged and her jaw dropped, she kept eating trying to ignore such a bizarre question.

"Yes, I do love Crystal, with all of my heart but not the way you might think kid. She is very special to me, but the timing has never been right and I suspect it never would have been. She is like a pain in the ass baby sister and that is the only way I will ever see her." He looked at Crystal then back to Bonaventura. "Besides, I had my true soul mate as you now have yours. Well kids, it is time to circle the wagons and prepare for attack."

Crystal looked up from her plate at Franco shaking her head. "Damn DeLuca, I keep waiting for you to shake me awake from this crazy dream I'm having." She

looked back and forth between him and Bonaventura.
"So what's our plan, guys?"

"Oh hell no. There is not going to be any *our* plan."
Bonaventura came to his feet wrapping an arm around
Crystal from behind. His arms stretched across her
collarbone he rested his chin on top of her head. "I love
that you want to help, but I cannot allow you to put
yourself in such peril."

Franco's eyes widened. He put his hand over his
mouth struggling to hold back a laugh as he watched for
Crystal to explode.

Crystal sucked in a deep breath. She pointed her fork
in her hand toward Franco. "You know better than to
pull that shit." She leaned back against Bonaventura's
chest craning her neck to look up at him. "You need to
learn that the surest way to get me involved in anything
is to tell me no. I know we are facing cat shit crazy, but
I could not live with myself if I just sat back and let the
two of you go it alone. We face this as a team or not at
all."

Bonaventura cupped her cheek in his hand. "I know you are a strong and brave woman, but Selena and Baldassare are not of your world." His words were soft and low.

"I fully understand." Crystal took his hand from her cheek kissing his palm. "You can give me one of those super stake thingies. I will have an angel and a prince at my side. Oh dear Lord, your father will be here soon. Now that scares the crap out of me."

Franco spoke up. "Me, too, Crystal. I expect Vettorio's arrival will be eventful to say the least." He leaned forward against the bar in front of them. "You can give it up kid. I have known that one for some time now and you will never change her mind. If she is not by our side, you can be sure she will be lurking around the corner somewhere, waiting to jump in." He locked on to Crystal's eyes. "I, too, am concerned for your safety, my dear. I wish you would sit this one out, but I do know better than to think such a thing could ever happen." He smiled and winked at her.

Crystal smiled back. "I promise you both I won't do anything stupid."

Franco got his jeans back on. The three of them stopped at Bonaventura's hotel room to get him a shirt. He had put on just his jacket after he showered at Crystal's. He grabbed the rest of the stakes he had brought with him then they went to Franco's house. They stuck closely together in his garage while teaching Crystal to use a crossbow. She picked it up quickly, as Franco knew she would.

Franco fashioned makeshift shells from two of the stakes using his shotgun shell re-loader.

Bonaventura picked up a shotgun from the rack hanging on the wall across from the workbench where Franco sat. "Sweet." He looked it over.

Franco called out without looking up. "Mossberg 500, 12 gauge, 18 1/2 inch barrel with a 3 inch

268

chamber. She'll hold six of these shells." He held up one

of the shells he had finished crafting. "Snap on that

pistol grip." Franco looked up pointing to the grip on a

shelf above Bonaventura. "And it will be tailor made for

dead eye dick over there." He nodded toward Crystal.

She stuck her tongue out at him.

"I am sorry but tell me, what is a dead eye dick?"

Bonaventura looked confused.

Crystal joined him. "He means I am an excellent

shot." She took the shotgun from his hands. "This is

sweet."

Franco pulled a set of keys from his pocket. Tossing

them to Bonaventura, "There is another one in the gun

safe. It's the tiny key with blue markings. The

combination is 04-17-18."

Bonaventura smirked. "The date of my birth?" He

opened the safe and retrieved the other shotgun

grinning wide.

"Don't go getting any ideas, junior. It was just easy

to remember," Franco grinned, "after over a thousand of

your epic celebrations your father held, who could forget?"

They spent several hours preparing their weapons. Bonaventura had never fired a gun so they decided Franco and Crystal would handle the shotguns and leave the crossbow and stakes to him. Before they knew it, the time had come to pick Vettorio up from the airport.

"Are you ready to face him?" Bonaventura asked Franco.

"Not really, but let's go and get it over with."

11

The King's Arrival

AFTER FLASHING THEIR BADGES TO
SECURITY FRANCO DROVE TO THE HANGER
WHERE VETTORIO'S JET WAS TO PARK. Their
timing was perfect. Vettorio's blue and white Honda-jet
had just touched down as they were climbing out of the
Nova.

"Nice ride." Franco looked at the shiny new jet
taxing toward them across the tarmac.

"Yea, he just got that one a few months ago."
Bonaventura deepened his voice mocking Vettorio. "It

was built in your neighboring North Carolina. It was the first one tested and released for sale, $4.5 mill and she is worth every penny." He chuckled lightly. "I personally see it as a means to get from point A to point B." Holding the front seat up, he offered Crystal his hand to help her out of the cramped back seat.

Franco closed the driver's door then leaned against it. A sudden flash of emotions ran through him: anxiety, a touch of fear and joy. The other two joined him.

Crystal leaned close taking Franco's hand with a slight smile she squeezed it tightly. "What is he like? Tell me all about the great king." She looked back and forth between the two men.

Franco spoke up. "He is a fair and just king. There were a few centuries there when I feared he had gone demon dark, but he came back from it." He looked at his feet, a sadness brought to his eyes by the memory.

"What do you mean by that?" Crystal asked.

"Go ahead; show her both sides to him." Bonaventura told him.

"A couple thousand years before junior came along, Vettorio went through a time where his humanity slipped away. He had finally come to realize his beloved Lilith was never coming for him. She was hiding out with Baldassare, the guy you met last night, and obviously had chosen him over Vettorio. He kind of went, as you like to say, bat shit crazy. He traveled across the Roman Empire, lying waste and taking up with various Germanic tribes." He hesitated. "Let's just say he acquired a taste for rather gruesome combat.

"He finally calmed down when he came to know Zenobia, she was a young widow, Queen of the Palmyrene Empire in Syria. Vettorio was her lover and confidant, of sorts. It is rumored their pillow talk led to her famous revolt against the Roman Empire." Franco shifted and looked up at the jet. It was at the far end of the runway circling around toward them.

"Tell me more about this queen. You can't leave me hanging. I am intrigued." Crystal tugged at his jacket.

Bonaventura picked up the story. "Julia Zenobia was well educated and spoke several languages. She was a

273

force to be reckoned with. Father actually admired her skills as a ruler. It was she that conquered Egypt and kicked out the Roman, Tenagino Probus. He had the balls to try and take the territory back from her. That cost him his head.

"She was beautiful, uniquely intelligent and equally dangerous with a dark complexion, pearly white teeth and eyes as black as a starless night. My father told me she was even more beautiful than her ancestor, Cleopatra, although she had a reputation for chastity, unlike Cleo. Her relationship with father was kept secret from her people." A tinge of excitement was evident in his voice as he recalled the story told to him by his father. "She rode a horse and hunted as well as any man and she had a taste for the drink." He snickered. "Father was very fond of her but he never really loved her and they parted ways with no ill regards. That was when he settled in what became Bozen, Italia, where he and my mother still make their home. I think that was around," He looked up searching to remember, "Oh yeah, around 273 AD."

The sound of the engine winding to a stop as the jet turned around in front of them brought a halt to the conversation. The three of them watched the green lights instantly turn red; the hanger bay doors began to open. The jet came to rest. Two men quickly pulled their truck in front of the jet and attached a hitch bar to the front axle, hastily backing the jet into the waiting hanger.

Crystal's mouth dropped open; her eyes grew to a guppy bulge. She washed her face with her hands and looked again for a second. "Holy shit Batman, *not* what I was expecting."

Vettorio stood in the open doorway as he made his exit from the jet. An air of sophistication and confidence rolled off him, lingering like a heavy fog. He could have stepped right out of the latest issue of Gentleman's Quarterly in his black Armani suit, crisp white shirt and tan raincoat. The overhead lights reflected off his blue eyes, chiseled check bones and way too hot handsome features. She felt her cheeks blush red and her knees nearly buckle. He barely looked a few years older than Vent; he certainly in no way looked to be anyone's dad.

Bonaventura put his arm around her, leaning in to whisper. "Smoldering good looks run in the family." He chuckled lightly at her reaction to Vettorio. "But remember love, my father is literally older than dirt." He pulled her closer, planting a kiss on her forehead. "You can roll your tongue back into your mouth now, *liebchen*."

Franco gave them a scornful gaze over his shoulder. "Seriously you two? Hush up."

Bonaventura let go of Crystal to grab Franco by his shoulders from behind as he stepped away from the car toward the plane. "You might want to let me go first, uncle."

"Good point, junior." Franco motioned him ahead and went back to stand next to Crystal.

Vettorio embraced his son in a bear hug. He released the hug catching Bonaventura by his upper arms in a firm grip with his hands, and placed a tender kiss on his forehead. "Are you all right my son?" He questioned.

Bonaventura nodded yes. Taking a step back, his eyes filled with parental concern, Vettorio let his hands slide down the length of his son's arms to his hands. Raising Bonaventura's hands in his own, he slowly turned his palms up. A deep growl began to rumble from his chest, the veins around his eyes surfaced and pulsed as he caught sight of the still healing wounds left from the staking. Baring his fangs, his growl grew into a feral scream with his eyes blazing.

Crystal could not hold back the gasp escaping her lips. She all but jumped into Franco's arms, hiding her face against his chest. He wrapped his arms around her, holding her tightly. With an open hand shielding the side of her face he calmed her in a low voice. "Shush, it's all right, Princess."

Vettorio snarled over his shoulder at Franco and Crystal before turning his attention back to his son. "This will not go unpunished, I assure you." He brought Bonaventura's hands to his lips, placing a kiss on each wound. Despite who and what he was, Vettorio had always been a warm and loving father.

"I am ashamed to have disappointed you, sire."

Bonaventura hung his head pulling his hands a way.

"Nonsense, you are my greatest pride, son. There is nothing you could ever do to tarnish my image of you. Now, if you will pardon me I have a personal matter to attend."

He turned on his heels and in a flash he had Franco separated from Crystal and pinned against the hanger wall with his right hand in a crushing grip around his throat. Franco did not resist, he held his arms widespread in the trust that Vettorio would calm down before he crushed his larynx.

Crystal had fallen to the pavement and was doing a crab crawl in terror backward, away from the two men.

Bonaventura wasted no time getting to her. He scooped her up in his arms calling out to Vettorio. "Father, please?"

Vettorio released his grip turning to Bonaventura. He gave Crystal a harsh gaze. "Is she the reason you have chosen to forsake me? To just disappear like a thief in the night and desert your family." He turned back to

Franco for his answer. "Tell me Michael. Help me understand why it is you would do such a thing, brother." He cocked his head to the side bloody tears forming in his eyes, voice anguished.

"No, Vettorio. Crystal had nothing to do with my decision. I know what I have done is unforgivable and maybe something you will never understand. I felt I had no choice other than to leave. After what Selena did to Bonaventura, I felt things shift in myself. I knew you would not allow me to kill her. My rage towards her was lethal and I knew it would be like killing you myself, if I harmed her. I know she is evil. I know you know this, as well but it does not change the fact she is your daughter. You have given her every chance of keeping herself alive. I could not abide by her almost killing her brother and you just banishing her. When I went on trips to your properties, I felt more at peace. I felt the rage leave me. When Bonaventura started going to opium dens, I knew it was time. I could no longer stand by on the sidelines and let him destroy himself. I tried, but he would not listen. He must get that from his father. I loved you

279

both so much that I didn't know if I could do it. I had to leave. I so wished I could tell you, but I knew a clean break was best for all involved.

"I went to Rome and looked into starting my own antique business. I still longed for the two of you and Althea. I was going to cave and come back to you and be forever in your service. That is when I met her. Her name was Maria and she was the most beautiful thing I had ever seen. I will not give you all the details, as this is not the time, but she became my world. This, I know you understand. I am sorry for all the pain I have put on you and your son. There is nothing else I can say or do for this."

"I slaughtered generations of people over my grief for you. I was inconsolable and Althea was worried over me. She thought I would never come back to her the way I was before. Over time, I have learned to put my grief behind me. I found my way again and enjoy my son and my family again. This is behind us now, as we have Selena to corral before more murders are committed. You are correct. I have a weakness in thinking she could be saved. I have learned I was wrong and must end her existence."

Franco snaked his arms around Vettorio's neck pulling him into a tearful embrace. The two men stood silently cheek-to-cheek, synchronized in their breathing for several minutes.

Then as they parted, Vettorio cocked his arm back and punched Franco so hard he flew several yards backwards. "Now we are even."

Bonaventura and Crystal were walking back to the car to give them some private time to talk things over. Crystal kept looking over Vent's shoulder, wondering if it was wise to leave the two men alone. She could literally taste the tension between them, but trusted Vent to know them better than she did. When she saw the punch and Franco flying through the air, she turned to run to him. Vent grabbed her around the waist and told her he would be okay. She needed to let it go. There were so many things she did not understand but this she did know, these men were dangerous and it was a damn good thing they were on her side.

281

12

Preparing For Battle

IT WAS TWO A.M. WHEN THEY ARRIVED BACK AT FRANCO'S PLACE. No one had spoken on the drive back. Bonaventura and Crystal were holding hands in the back seat, neither daring to be the first to speak. Sleet began popping against the metal roof of the garage, echoing inside like popcorn bursting open as the Nova rolled to a stop.

As soon as they had all departed the car Vettorio pulled off his raincoat and suit jacket and rolled up his sleeves. He turned around looking at Bonaventura and Crystal who were hovering in a corner. "I know you were raised with proper manners. Are you not going to make an introduction?"

"Yes sir, I do apologize." He placed an open hand on Crystal's back, guiding her toward his father. After nearly twelve hundred years his father still had the ability to make him feel five years old. A gentle smile curled on his lips. "May I introduce Crystal Harley father?" He cleared his throat and his smile spread across his face. "In the midst of madness, I have found my soul mate." His smile disappeared as he diverted his eyes to the floor. "You should know, Selena has sworn to take her from me in a manner the likes of which I shall not repeat."

An inauspicious look took over Vettorio's soft features. "We shall have to see to it that plan does not come to fruition, son."

Crystal felt a slight shiver go up her spine. He took her by the hand. His touch was cool but not as cold as she had expected and his hand was soft and smooth.

Crystal thought his hand would feel like her grandmother's had when she held it at her funeral. He placed a chaste kiss in her palm and then raised her hand spinning her slowly in a circle in front of him before she could respond. "Well then young lady, it is my honor to make your acquaintance." He replaced his dark expression with a warm smile and an arched brow.

"The honor is mine, your majesty." Crystal bobbed a curtsy at him trying not to giggle.

Vettorio laughed. "You needn't be so formal *demoiselle*, please call me King." He tossed an approving look to Bonaventura, holding Crystal's hand in his open palm with a gesture for his son to take it.

Bonaventura wasted no time in doing so. He shook his head, taking her hand in his and pulling her close to his side. "Forgive my father's lame attempt at humor."

Vettorio winked at Crystal, "Just call me Vettorio child." He walked to the Nova.

"Bonaventura and Crystal followed Vettorio to the trunk where he took out a long leather case and his overnight bag. He shut the trunk, sat the overnight bag on the floor and placed the leather case with great care on the workbench near Franco. Opening it, he gave Crystal a detailed description as he unsheathed the finely honed ten thousand year old, one-of-its-kind hand-sword. The twenty-four inch blade and its hilt were cast as one solid piece from a base of arsenic copper and meteor iron. The fuller, beautifully inlaid with the image of the great dragon Nidhugin in pure silver, a tiny ruby on either side for his eyes. The blade was plated with a mix of titanium and platinum, while the tip was covered with a rare ancient form of rhodium. The grip bound by red silk. A platinum and silver rapier style guard fanned out around the hilt coming together at the biggest emerald Crystal had ever seen forming its pommel. Vettorio held the sword in front of Crystal in open palms "After my blacksmith fashioned the sword it was placed standing upright in a mound. Thor cast down a lightning bolt creating a magical weapon to be used only against the vilest of evil creatures. To raise it against an undeserving soul would bring certain death to whoever wielded it."

Crystal was very entranced by his story. Franco and Bonaventura were both greatly enjoying watching her childlike expressions as she hung on every word, her mouth slightly a gap.

"I shall relieve Baldassare of his head, sending him to hell once and for all." Vettorio took Crystal's hand, placing it around the delicate silk grip before stepping back. Her eyes widened to their limits, she sucked in a deep breath. He walked behind her, reaching his arms around Crystal he placed his hands against the tops of hers, guiding her to raise the blade upright in her hands. "Can you feel the magic? The power?" He whispered over her shoulder. She nodded her head, still holding her breath.

Franco spoke up, "Magical indeed, I think the impossible has occurred. I have never seen Miss Harley struck speechless." He smirked.

She snapped out of her trance, laughed a good sarcastic laugh, and called him an ass. Instantly, she whipped her head in the direction of Vettorio and apologized. Vettorio laughed as well and told her not to apologize for Michael was, in fact, an ass. After more tutorials on the sword and its blade, they decided to call it a night and get the rest they were going to need.

The next day was spent reviewing what plan worked best with a variety of possible scenarios. The tension was building. Everyone was aware of the dire situation at hand. It would be hardest on Vettorio. No matter how she had turned out, Selena was his child. They had shared a blood link for thousands of years. Franco told him he and Bonaventura would deal with Selena and Vettorio should focus on Baldassare.

Crystal waved her hand in the air. "Hello, don't forget about me. I am right here."

"You, young lady are to stick by my side at all times." Vettorio answered. He checked his watch. It was going on five o'clock and the sun was going down.

Having been informed of Crystal's stubborn streak, and her intentions to join them back at her house to face Baldassare and Selena, Vettorio made the decision to glamour her into staying put. He knew his son would be hard pressed to win her forgiveness if he dared to glamour her should she ever find out. It was a necessary trick to shield her from Selena. Crystal would surely be her first target once it was apparent the angel and king were there to stand fast beside Bonaventura against her. He knew the workings of her mind well. She would want to insure Crystal met her death in plain view of Bonaventura, even if it sealed her own fate. Vettorio instructed Crystal to go into the house, enjoy a long hot bath then find a restful sleep in Franco's guest bedroom. "Drift off to sleep with visions of riding a pure white steed, among sweet woodland fairies, deep in the forest, with the sound of a waterfall tumbling into a lake."

Bonaventura and Franco tossed him a look in unison. He shrugged his shoulders and smiled at them before leading her inside Franco's house. Vettorio made sure he heard the water running and chuckled a bit

289

when he heard Crystal humming a sweet tune before he went back outside to the two who awaited him.

Bonaventura and Franco were both leaning against the Nova, arms crossed over their chests when Vettorio returned to the garage. Catching the look they were still darting at him, he threw his hands up, "What? One of us had to do it."

"Was the whole woodland fairy thing necessary, father?" He shook his head. "She is going to be so pissed off. If we live, you will need to make her forget the entire Selena thing or she may end me herself."

"I thought it was a nice touch." Franco laughed. "But you are correct in thinking she may kill you later. That one there, she is most definitely what the Americans call full of piss and vinegar."

Vettorio squeezed in between them. "As much as I hate to bring it up, we might as well get on with it." The laughter from a moment before was gone, instantly replaced with heavy hearts and a somber mood. He spread his arms around Franco and Bonaventura, his open palms against the far side of their heads. Pulling them one at a time toward him, he kissed them on the cheek. "I wish to have a say before we leave this place. Should we not return, I want the two of you to know you have always lived in my heart," he tapped his hand to his chest, "right here next to my beloved Althea."

He turned to Franco, taking his face in his hands. He leaned in so that they were touching foreheads. "I hold no ill will in my heart toward you Michael, Franco. I have given careful consideration of what my own actions may have been had I felt I must choose between Althea and you. I cannot say without any doubt that I would not have done the same." The two men embraced for a long while. They were barely moving or breathing. Vent gave them the space they needed and felt his heart lighten at his father's words and actions. He knew what it meant to both of them and to him. Vent could not help the tears pooling in his eyes, but was grateful they were not seen.

The sleet had finally stopped, leaving a thin sheet of ice twinkling on the ground under the bright full moon. In the silence, the crunch of their footsteps in the ice echoed across Crystal's lawn as they made their way to the house. Once inside they spread their arsenal out on the dining room table.

Vettorio pulled his sword from its sheath. Staring at the blade, his mind drifted back to the night he met Selena. She was such a rare beauty, full of fire and a gifted musician. He was attending a symposium in Athens, Greece. Slave girls had come around and washed the hands of the men around the table once the meal had been consumed. The room was then swept clean, and splashed with perfume. Garlands were presented for the men to wear before they moved from the table to couches lined up against the wall for them to lounge in.

It was time to drink and enjoy the night's entertainment. Vettorio had dipped his cup into the wine bowl many times before she entered the hall and began to play her flute. He was strangely aroused by her playing as she worked her way around the room in a Pan like rhythm. Many had set their sights on taking her, but it was he that took her to his bed as night was overtaken by the rising sun.

She was his first.

He had taken her tender ivory neck into his mouth. In the heat of passion he sank his fangs deep; the taste of her blood was so intoxicating that he hadn't wanted to release her until every drop had slid down the back of his throat. He had almost drained her when he came to his senses. It was she that begged him to make her immortal like him. He had been terribly lonely. The few friends he had made over the years had grown old and died. He thought it might be time to make an immortal family of his own.

"Are you all right?" Franco's voice brought him back to the present. Vettorio blinked eyes filled with despair and nodded.

It was nearing ten o'clock when Selena and Baldassare made their way past the marsh's edge into Crystal's back yard. She held her hand out for him to stop. Raising her nose in the air, she was taken aback by the scents coming from inside the house. She looked up at Baldassare. "Father is here and I smell the stench of an angel. Are you prepared to face him?" She scowled.

"I am." Baldassare rolled his shoulders back puffing his chest out. He tilted his head from side to side quickly, producing a knuckle cracking sound from the bones in his neck. "I have waited much too long for this." He curled his upper lip.

Selena was not so anxious to face Bonaventura anymore. Not with the others in there to defend him.

She did not have a death wish but pride would not allow her to back down, so she pushed onward. She knew her father would be alerted to her presence and she felt her mind taunting him to come out and face her.

Vettorio was the first to know they were outside. He motioned to Franco.

"Yeah, I can feel them." Franco picked up the shotgun bracing him against the wall.

Bonaventura, with crossbow in hand nodded to his father then flashed to peek out the window. He watched as Selena waved Baldassare ahead of her to face them first. He thought that so typical of her to have him shield her. He was determined it would do her no good. She had threatened Crystal virulently thereby signing her own death warrant, as far he was concerned. The time had come to send his sister to Asgard for the gods to pass judgment on her and no doubt cast her into hell.

He turned, signaling to Franco that the two were approaching the back door.

Franco acknowledged him. He shimmied out of his shirt. With a snap, his wings unfurled. He exchanged a knowing look with Vettorio.

The back door flew open and Baldassare entered pulling his sword from its sheath hanging on his back. He went straight for Vettorio. In an instant, the sound of blade against blade filled the room. The two angels fallen from grace were equally matched. Baldassare's blade was the first to make contact, ripping through the flesh on Vettorio's left bicep.

Selena flashed in. Franco took a shot at her but missed. Her face flushed with incredulity as their eyes locked on one another. She knew there was an angel inside but had not recognized it as Michael. She ran at him baring her fangs through a banshee cry.

Bonaventura launched a bolt from his crossbow that fell short. Selena snarled at him over her shoulder before reaching Franco. She caught him by the throat. The two of them hit the floor rolling in a fit of fangs with feathers flying. Bonaventura pulled another bolt from the tube, struggling to take aim not to hit Franco. He squeezed the trigger. The bolt struck her in the calf, but went clean through. She screamed, grabbing the wound. It was painful but not debilitating. She flashed out the door. Franco gave chase behind her.

Vettorio and Baldassare were still exchanging blows. Both of them were rife with bloody gashes on their arms and legs. Baldassare landed a blow behind Vittorio's knee that sliced through his cruciate ligament bringing him to his knees on the floor and giving him the clear shot he needed. Vettorio's sword fell from his grip to the floor.

Baldassare pulled back his sword ready to remove Vettorio's head when Bonaventura flashed to grab his father's sword. Raising the sword above his head in one fell swoop he lowered the blade with all his might, slicing clean through Baldassare's neck between his C4 and C5 vertebrae. His head hit the heart-pine floor with a thump. His body fell in a heap. Baldassare looked up at Bonaventura, blinked three times and it was over.

Eyes frozen wide in death, the once angel, and now demon began to disintegrate.

Suddenly, Bonaventura was being engulfed in a blinding white light, excruciating pain bounced around inside of him. Vettorio looked on in awe with no idea what was happening to his son or what he could do to help him. Bonaventura ripped his shirt away from his body. He pawed at his back growling out in pain. Vettorio stood and came closer standing in front of him taking Bonaventura's hands in his, locking their fingers together as his son went to his knees. Vettorio sucked in a breath, his eyes widened in disbelief as he witnessed the unimaginable. Bonaventura screamed out, his eyes rolled back in his head and sweat beaded up on his forehead. A pair of black wings sprang free unfurling wide from his son. Vettorio wept at the sight of the dark angel. He let go of his son's hands, fell to his knees and wrapped his arms around his neck kissing his cheek. "By the gods you have been blessed my son."

Bonaventura looked up to his father's face with confusion at his words and promptly passed out.

Vettorio cradled him for several moments before he heard movement outside the house and he stood to ready himself to defend his son in his time of ultimate need.

Thankfully, it was Michael who rushed through the door, stating she was gone. He stopped in the doorway awe struck by the sight of Bonaventura with the dark angel wings. "Wow, I can't leave you alone for a minute," he blurted out for a lack of anything else to say. He approached the two of them as Vettorio fell back to his knees to cradle his son that was coming to. Franco looked at the bloody sword lying next to Bonaventura, then the pile of ash that had been Baldassare. "So now you are packing feathers, kid." Franco let out a nervous laugh. He helped them both to their feet. Vettorio's wounds were nearly healed already.

"Come, we must find her." Vettorio proclaimed heading outside.

Bonaventura was still dumb struck by what had just happened to him. He shook it off, retracted his wings and followed his father and Franco out the door.

Franco, Vettorio and Bonaventura searched the marsh and the beach until nearly dawn, but found no sign of Selena. She had escaped with merely a flesh wound in her calf. Their hopes to be rid of her had been within reach but slipped away like the outgoing tide.

Bonaventura had a sudden sense of foreboding that shook him to the core. "Crystal. I have to get to her. I have a horrible feeling."

When the three men arrived back at Franco's house the front door was lying on the steps, obviously ripped off the hinges and thrown in anger by Selena. Bonaventura was the first to reach the bedroom. Crystal was barely breathing. Her body nearly ripped to shreds left to die in a bloody pool. "Oh by the god's blood." Bonaventura cried out falling to his knees next to the bed. He gently slid a hand under her head, pushing bloody strands of hair away from her face with the other hand. Vettorio placed a caring hand on his shoulder. "Father, I can't lose her." Bonaventura looked up at Vettorio with pleading eyes filled with bloody tears.

Franco went to the other side of the bed and started accessing the extent of her wounds. "This is not good kid, not good at all." He choked back a lump in his throat looking at Crystal covered in so much blood. "We may be able to save her. It will take all of our powers together." He looked at Bonaventura eye to eye.

"But I have no idea what powers I have or how the fuck to use them."

"Your grace will take over and guide you. Trust me on this kid." Franco pleaded.

"He's right son, the two of you can do this, or you could turn her now before she dies." Vettorio gripped his shoulder.

"No, I don't want it to be like this, she has to want to be my mate of her own free will." Letting her head rest against the bed Bonaventura stood up. "What do I do?"

"First we call out our wings." Franco instructed.

"How?" Bonaventura asked with a mournful plea in his eyes.

"Close your eyes and focus. See your wings appearing in your mind and they will obey."

Within moments, both of them stood on either side of the bed with wings unfurled fully. Franco kneeled down sliding his hands under Crystal. Bonaventura followed suit. She was levitated slightly off the bed, the light from their grace emanated from beneath her body. Vettorio stood at the foot of the bed, head bowed.

The two angels, light and dark prayed to the gods to heal her wounds. Strong lightning strikes licked against the windows. Thunder roared so hard the house shook beneath its power.

Crystal was slowly lowered back on the bed. Her wounds began closing one by one. Franco nodded to Bonaventura and they both smiled lightly.

Crystal opened her eyes. Looking around at the three men, a tiny gasp then cough escaped her lips as she forced her tongue to make words. "Holy shit, am I dead?" She asked.

Franco burst out in laughter, "Our girl is back."

Vent broke out into racking sobs laced with laughter. He clung to Crystal and would not let go.

She was confused and tried to struggle out of Vent's grip. "Hey. Hey! Why the tears? What's going on?"

Bonaventura let her go and simply explained what had happened. She was instantly enthralled with anger when she learned she was glamoured. However, when she heard what the men had come back to and the state she was in.

She began to feel around her body, making sure all was, in fact, intact and then lunged back into Vent's arms. "I'm sorry you had to do that and think you were going to lose me. Thank you both for saving my life. I should be pissed and more than likely will be a bit later, but right now I am only thankful. I love you, so much." She leaned into him and he wrapped her in his arms once more.

The ringing of Vettorio's cell phone interrupted the silence in the room. "What do you mean she is gone? By the god's blood if any thing has happened to my wife this world will not survive my wrath."

All eyes went to him with concern as they watched his eyes blaze red and the veins begin to protrude with growing rage. He snapped the phone shut, sending it across the room so hard it went through the bedroom door before shattering into pieces.

Vettorio let out a deep growl so fierce the glass of the window behind him cracked. With bloody tears staining his face, he looked at his son. "Selena has taken your mother."

End of Part One

* Please continue on to the quoted poems, and a

peek at book 2

Norse Poems

Valhalla

When questioned concerning the creation of the world, the Northern scalds, or poets, whose songs are preserved in the Eddas and Sagas, declared that in the beginning, when there was as yet no Earth, nor sea, nor air, when darkness rested over all, there existed a powerful being called Allfather, whom they dimly conceived as uncreated as well as unseen, and that whatever he willed came to pass.

In the centre of space there was, in the morning of time, a great abyss called Ginnunga-gap, the cleft of clefts, the yawning gulf, whose depths no eye could fathom, as it was enveloped in perpetual twilight. North of this abode was a space or world known as Niflheim, the home of mist and darkness, in the centre of which bubbled the exhaustless spring Hvergelmir, the seething cauldron, whose waters supplied twelve great streams known as the Elivagar. As the water of these streams flowed swiftly away from its source and encountered the cold blasts from the yawning gulf, it soon hardened into huge blocks of ice, which rolled downward into the immeasurable depths of the great abyss with a continual roar like thunder.

South of this dark chasm, and directly opposite Niflheim, the realm of mist, was another world called Muspells-heim, the home of elemental fire, where all was warmth and brightness, and whose frontiers were continually guarded by Surt, the flame giant. This giant fiercely brandished his flashing sword, and continually sent forth great showers of sparks, which fell with a hissing sound upon the ice-blocks in the bottom of the

abyss, and partly melted them by their heat.

"Great Surtur, with his burning sword,

Southward at Muspel's gate kept ward,

And flashes of celestial flame,

Life-giving, from the fire-world came." *Valhalla (JC Jones)*

Ymir and Audhumla

As the steam rose in clouds it again encountered the prevailing cold, and was changed into rime or hoarfrost, which, layer by layer, filled up the great central space. Thus by the continual action of cold and heat, and also probably by the will of the uncreated and unseen, a gigantic creature called Ymir or Orgelmir (seething clay), the personification of the frozen ocean, came to life amid the ice-blocks in the abyss, and as he was born of rime he was called a Hrim-thurs, or ice-giant.

"In early times,
When Ymir lived,
Was sand, nor sea,
Nor cooling wave;

No Earth was found,

Nor heaven above;

One chaos all,

And nowhere grass."

Saemund's Edda (Henderson's tr.).

Groping about in the gloom in search of something to eat, Ymir perceived a gigantic cow called Audhumla (the nourisher), which had been created by the same agency as himself, and out of the same materials. Hastening towards her, Ymir noticed with pleasure that from her udder flowed four great streams of milk, which would supply ample nourishment.

All his wants were thus satisfied; but the cow, looking about her for food in her turn, began to lick the salt off a neighbouring ice-block with her rough tongue. This she continued to do until first the hair of a god appeared and then the whole head emerged from its icy envelope, until by-and-by Buri (the producer) stepped forth entirely free.

While the cow had been thus engaged, Ymir, the [ ]giant, had fallen asleep, and as he slept a son and daughter were born from the perspiration under his armpit, and his feet produced the six-headed giant Thrudgelmir, who, shortly after his birth, brought forth in his turn the giant Bergelmir, from whom all the evil frost giants are descended.

"Under the armpit grew,

'Tis said of Hrim-thurs,

A girl and boy together;

Foot with foot begat,

Of that wise Jötun,

A six-headed son." Saemund's Edda (Thorpe's TR.)

Odin, Vili, and Ve

When these giants became aware of the existence of the god Buri, and of his son Börr (born), whom he had immediately produced, they began waging war against them, for as the gods and giants represented the opposite forces of good and evil, there was no hope of their living together in peace. The struggle continued evidently for ages, neither party gaining a decided advantage, until Börr married the giantess Bestla, daughter of Bolthorn (the thorn of evil), who bore him three powerful sons, Odin (spirit), Vili (will), and Ve (holy). These three sons immediately joined their father in his struggle against the hostile frost-giants, and finally succeeded in slaying their deadliest foe, the great Ymir. As he sank down lifeless the blood gushed from his wounds in such floods that it produced a great deluge, in which all his race perished, with the exception of Bergelmir, who escaped in a boat and went with his wife to the confines of the world.

"And all the race of Ymir thou didst drown,

Save one, Bergelmer: he on shipboard fled

Thy deluge, and from him the giants sprang."

Balder Dead (Matthew Arnold).

Here he took up his abode, calling the place Jötunheim (the home of the giants), and here he begat a new race of frost-giants, who inherited his dislikes, continued the feud, and were always ready to sally forth from their desolate country and raid the territory of the gods.

The gods, in Northern mythology called Aesir (pillars and supporters of the world), having thus triumphed over their foes, and being no longer engaged in perpetual warfare, now began to look about them, with intent to improve the desolate aspect of things and fashion a habitable world. After due consideration

313

Börr's sons rolled Ymir's great corpse into the yawning

abyss, and began to create the world out of its various

component parts.

The Creation of the Earth

Out of the flesh they fashioned Midgard (middle garden), as the Earth was called. This was placed in the exact centre of the vast space, and hedged all round with Ymir's eyebrows for bulwarks or ramparts. The solid portion of Midgard was surrounded by the giant's blood or sweat, which formed the ocean, while his bones made the hills, his flat teeth the cliffs, and his curly hair the trees and all vegetation.

Well pleased with the result of their first efforts at creation, the gods now took the giant's unwieldy skull and poised it skillfully as the vaulted heavens above Earth and sea; then scattering his brains throughout the expanse beneath they fashioned from them the fleecy clouds.

"Of Ymir's flesh

Was Earth created,

Of his blood the sea,

Of his bones the hills,

Of his hair trees and plants,

Of his skull the heavens,

And of his brows

The gentle powers

Formed Midgard for the sons of men;

But of his brain

The heavy clouds are

All created." Norse Mythology (R. B. Anderson).

To support the heavenly vault, the gods stationed the strong dwarfs, Nordri, Sudri, Austri, Westri, at its four corners, bidding them sustain it upon their shoulders, and from them the four points of the compass received their present names of North, South, East, and West. To give light to the world thus created, the gods studded the heavenly vault with sparks secured from Muspells-heim, points of light which shone steadily through the gloom like brilliant stars. The most vivid of these sparks, however, were reserved for the manufacture of the sun and moon, which were placed in beautiful golden chariots.

"And from the flaming world, where Muspel reigns,

Thou sent'st and fetched'st fire, and madest lights:

Sun, moon, and stars, which thou hast hung in heaven,

Dividing clear the paths of night and day." *Balder Dead (Matthew Arnold).*

When all these preparations had been finished, and the steeds Arvakr (the early waker) and Alsvin (the rapid goer) were harnessed to the sun-chariot, the gods, fearing lest the animals should suffer from their proximity to the ardent sphere, placed under their withers great skins filled with air or with some refrigerant substance. They also fashioned the shield Svalin (the cooler), and placed it in front of the car to shelter them from the sun's direct rays, which would else

317

have burned them and the Earth to a cinder. The

moon-car was, similarly, provided with a fleet steed

called Alsvider (the all-swift); but no shield was required

to protect him from the mild rays of the moon.

Book 2

The Dark Prince and the Angel Chronicles saga continues with the next installment of... The Quest for Selena

Selena had no problem controlling Vettorio's human pilot. It took only seconds for her to glamour him to file a flight plan and in a short while they were off to Bozen, Italy. She instructed him to refuel and file a flight plan to Moscow while she quickly made her way to Vettorio's castle.

Althea was resting in her greenhouse. Stretched out in her favorite chaise among the flowers she was deep in thought looking up at the snow falling against the glass ceiling. Selena appeared standing over her smirking. In one fell swoop Selena plunged a silver danger into Althea's heart disabling her enough for Selena to bind her hands in makeshift handcuffs made of flexible tender new growth from the world tree, an original's kryptonite.

She will take her to Russia where she ditches the jet and with the aid of one of her deviant dens she leaves there by train. Selena makes several stops around Europe before deciding she has covered her trail.

Will Vettorio, Bonaventura and Michael find them and in time to prevent permanent hard to Althea? Will Selena meet her final death once and for all?

Spoiler alert... there will be another wedding at the castle.

Dear Readers, friends and fans

Thank you from the bottom of my heart for all of the support and encouragement you have given me.

I hope that you enjoyed part one of The Dark Prince and the Angel Chronicles. Please leave an honest review on all venues, Amazon , https://www.goodreads.com/

Feel free to contact me anytime, I love to hear from you. Email wisej5875@gmail.com *
http://www.facebook.com/crystalsunicorn or twitter
https://twitter.com/CrystalsUnicorn